The Village Gossip

By

Timothy Shay Arthur

©2013 Bottom of the Hill Publishing
All rights reserved. No part of this book may be used or reproduced in any manner without written permission except for brief quotations for review purposes only.
This book was written in the prevailing style of that period. Language and spelling have been left original in an effort to give the full flavor of this classic work.

Bottom of the Hill Publishing
Memphis, TN
www.BottomoftheHillPublishing.com

ISBN: 978-1-4837-0029-8

The Village Gossip

"At the same time they also learn to be idle, as they go around from house to house; and not merely idle, but also *gossips* and busybodies, talking about things not proper to mention!" 1 Timothy 5:13

Content

CHAPTER 1	9
CHAPTER 2	15
CHAPTER 3	23
CHAPTER 4	29
CHAPTER 5	33
CHAPTER 6	41
CHAPTER 7	47
CHAPTER 8	55
CHAPTER 9	63
CHAPTER 10	69
CHAPTER 11	77
CHAPTER 12	83
CHAPTER 13	91
CHAPTER 14	99

CHAPTER 1

A pleasanter village than *Cedardale* could hardly be found. Nearly environed by wooded hills, a lively imagination would have called it a bird's nest; and its snow-white cottages, the beautiful eggs.

Nature had done everything for Cedardale; and if the hearts of its few inhabitants had been as much in *harmony* with what was good and lovely as the scenery around them — the place would have been a *little Paradise*.

But such *harmony* was not in Cedardale. Do we find it anywhere? What is the sighing answer? "No!" Not as the clear stream that went gliding, rippling, and singing happily on its way through the village — working cheerfully for the gray old miller, after taking a little rest in the broad mill-dam, and then pressing onward to give life and freshness to green meadows, or to gather again its strength for toiling man — not, we say, as this clear stream did the current of life in Cedardale receive, and give back the sunlight. No, no. This *life-current* went ever fretting on, turbid, restless, and impatient — marring its banks, and seeking rather to do evil than good.

There was no harmony nor mutual interests, no unselfish regard the one for the other. If each did not seek to do his neighbor *wrong*, there was in the mind of each a *fear* of his neighbor. Suspicion, jealousy, ill-will, and mutual dislike — were kept alive from month to month, and from year to year. Not that the inhabitants of Cedardale were more suspicious, jealous, and ill-natured than other people. No, this was not the reason. What was it, then? We shall see.

There was in Cedardale a mill, and, as a matter of course, a miller. The miller was somewhat advanced in years — say, past sixty. His name was Stephen White. Now the miller was rather a quick-tempered man, and hasty of speech; and what was worse, this infirmity increased with his years. So it is with every disease of the body and mind; if it is not removed in early manhood or middle age — it will increase as we grow old! In consequence of this infirmity, the miller was all the time *in hot water*, as they say, *with somebody*.

Still, our friend the miller would have passed along far more comfortably to himself and his neighbors, if it hadn't been for Wimble the shoemaker, and his wife Nancy — the shoemaker's wife, we mean. Nancy Wimble was the *busybody, tattler,* and *mischief-maker* of the village; and her husband, a good, easy sort of man at first — had insensibly fallen into her bad habit of *minding other people's business,* more than his own. "As the old rooster crows — the young one learns." So says the proverb; and it was true in the case of Wimble's *children.* They were the most inveterate *meddlers* in what did not concern them, to be found; even not, at times, excepting their mother. It was this family, in fact, that set all the rest of the village on fire, and made of lovely little Cedardale as uncomfortable a place, as a quiet peace-loving man could wish to live in.

Martin, the village schoolmaster, a weak, but well-meaning man, had his own time of it. This may readily be inferred, when it is known that he had been bold enough to turn *Dick Wimble* out of school for bad conduct. Dick was certainly the *worst boy* in Cedardale, and the most *troublesome* fellow that Martin had to deal with. He had deserved expulsion twenty times, before the schoolmaster's indignation made him regardless of all the consequences to be feared from the anger of Nancy Wimble. The last outrage upon his dignity as schoolmaster, which brought upon Dick the penalty of expulsion, was in this way. Martin had found it necessary to forbid, positively, the bringing of fruit into the school. At first the prohibition extended only to the eating of fruit during school-hours. But this not meeting the evil he sought to remedy — as the boys, with fruit in their desks or pockets, would be tempted to eat it stealthily, under the hope of escaping detection by the master — he made the more sweeping edict which forbade its being brought into the school-room at all.

Regardless of this, Dick, on the very next day after the law was announced, brought a large red apple in his pocket. While he was in the act of passing it into his desk, Martin's eye caught the glow of one of its ruddy cheeks.

"Dick!" he called out in a voice so sharp and stern, that young Wimble gave a startle and let the apple fall upon the floor.

"Come here, sir!" said the schoolmaster.

Dick obeyed the summons with pouting lips and a frowning brow.

"Go back and get me the apple," said Martin.

The apple was brought. It was large, ripe, and mellow; and, as

Dick resigned it to the schoolmaster, he felt more grief at the loss of the fruit, than fear of personal consequences.

"Now, hold out your hand." The schoolmaster raised his ruler.

Dick at first hesitated, but the loud, angry, "Do you hear me, sir!" brought his arm into a horizontal position, and his palm exposed to the master's view.

Two or three quick strokes followed, and then the lad was sent to his seat.

Martin placed the apple on his desk, in view of the school, where it remained until about half-past eleven o'clock. Then the spicy fragrance, which had come ever to his nostrils, tempted him to take it in his hand, pare it with his knife, and deliberately eat it in presence of the scholars, unwisely using, as he did so, language that Dick Wimble felt as tantalizing.

"I'll get him for it!" said the boy to himself. "See if I don't. He took my apple just to eat it himself, so he did. But he'll be sorry for it, or I'm mistaken!"

Martin certainly committed an error, in thus eating the apple.

"If it is wrong for us to eat apples in school, it is wrong for him," said the boys, as they clustered together on the play-ground, after dismissal.

Dick told his story at home, and in his own way. The most important fact, the *order* not to bring fruit to school, he was very careful to hide. So, all that his father and mother understood was, that Martin had taken away their son's apple, and greedily eaten it himself in the presence of the whole school.

"I'd get even with him for it," said Mrs. Wimble, thoughtlessly.

"And I will, too," was Dick's prompt answer. "He shall not have my apples for nothing!"

"I'll tell you a good trick to play off on him," remarked Dick's father, chuckling to himself as he spoke.

"What's that?" quickly asked the lad.

"I don't know that I ought to tell you," said Mr. Wimble.

"Oh yes, father, do," urged Dick. "Now, what is it?"

The shoemaker had thought twice — a thing not very common with him before speaking. Generally, he spoke first and thought afterwards. So he replied —

"You know enough mischief already, Dick, without my putting any more into your head."

"Ah, do tell me now, won't you? I want to know so bad. Is it to put a *crooked pin* in his chair?"

"Oh, no."

"To bore a hole in the bottom of his chair, and fix a pin under it with a string to my desk?"

"No — no. Nothing of that kind."

"What is it, then? Won't you tell me?"

And so the boy urged and urged his father, until the latter, to get rid of his importunities, finally imparted the *secret* he wished to know.

Dick now fairly danced with delight. Oh, it was such a good trick! he said over and over again; and he would play it off on the schoolmaster, even if he got killed for it.

The shoemaker rather discouraged his son; but the lad was resolved to "pay the schoolmaster back again."

On the next morning, when Dick started for school, he had in his pocket a beautiful large apple, ripe, mellow, and tempting to behold. This he managed to slip into his desk so dexterously that the schoolmaster's eye failed to note its presence. School had been in about an hour when Dick opened his desk, and taking his apple in his hand, exposed it so far that it was seen by Martin.

"Dick Wimble!" The schoolmaster's voice showed that he felt a sudden strong anger at the hardihood and persistent disobedience of the boy. "Bring me that apple. How dare you do so after what passed yesterday!"

Dick, willing to take some good whacks with the ruler in view of his anticipated retaliation, went up to the schoolmaster's desk with a light step, gave him the apple, and received in turn five hard strokes on the hand.

The apple, as on the day before, was placed by Martin on his desk, where it remained for about an hour. Then he took it up and said aloud, with something tantalizing in his voice —

"A very fine apple indeed. Where did this grow, Dick? On one of your father's trees?"

"Yes, sir," replied the boy, turning around from his desk and looking at the schoolmaster; a movement in which he was imitated by the whole school.

"I'm sorry you didn't eat it at home, my lad," resumed the schoolmaster, "then you would have had a double pleasure — the pleasure of taste, and the reflection that you had disobeyed no rule. As it is, I must eat this nice apple for you."

And as Martin said this he raised the apple, from which he had removed a small portion of the skin, and took a mouthful from it. At the moment of doing so, there was a puff of something into his face, eyes, and nostrils, which he at once perceived to be *cayenne pepper*. The truth was, Dick had dexterously filled a cavity which he had scooped out of the apple with about a thimbleful of very fine dry pepper, and it so happened that the schoolmaster sprung this *mine* at the first bite. The young rebel could not refrain from a hearty burst of laughter at the success of his trick; and in this he was joined by nearly the whole school.

In due time, Martin got his eyes clear of the pepper, and in due time Dick got a terrible flogging, after which he was formally expelled from the school.

This expulsion was rather more than the shoemaker and his wife, who knew what their son was about to do, anticipated; and as the act was regarded by them as a most uncalled-for exercise of power, they forthwith paid a visit to the schoolmaster, and demanded to have Dick taken back. Martin declared that the boy would never darken the school-room door again.

"In that case, very few boys will darken it in three months from now, let me tell you for your comfort," retorted Nancy Wimble.

Martin had cause to know and fear this woman's *baneful* influence; and her threat not only disturbed him, but made him waver in his purpose. Her remark soon after, that there would be another schoolmaster in Cedardale before six months, decided the debate which had arisen in his mind. Some further parley ensued, and then, with a very bad grace, he consented to let Dick come back again into the school. The lad, conscious of having *triumphed* over the master, was *more troublesome* and *rebellious* than ever.

We have said that Martin had his own time of it in Cedardale; and the reader can easily understand, from this little digression, why it was so. Nancy Wimble never forgave him for turning Dick out of school, and consequently never failed to speak ill of him when an opportunity for doing so offered.

Besides the miller, schoolmaster, and shoemaker — another prominent personage was *Striker*, the *blacksmith*, a good mechanic in his way, but a very hard drinker. He did not meddle himself much in other people's affairs, though some in the village took a great deal of interest in his; and, in their ill-directed efforts to reform him, riveted, rather than loosened, the terrible chains by which the *monster intemperance* had bound him.

These were the leading personages in Cedardale — the miller, the shoemaker, the schoolmaster, and the blacksmith; and in their jealousies and antagonisms, they managed to keep the little community of which they formed a part, nearly the whole time in hot water.

In an adjoining village, some two miles distant, resided one *Mr. Sharp*, a selfish, unscrupulous, cunning *lawyer*, who managed most adroitly to get up, every year, some two or three profitable *disputes* among his neighbors. One farmer, who owned two or three hundred acres of good land, he had induced to enter into a lawsuit about the *right of way* claimed by a neighboring farmer, across a narrow strip of his land. The result was, three years of trouble in the courts, the loss of his case, finally, and the sacrifice of nearly everything he was worth, to pay costs and fees. Some others had suffered nearly as much from a like cause — but Sharp put money in his pocket, and encouraged others to imitate the bad example.

Up to the time when our story begins, Sharp had failed to get a case in Cedardale, although he had tried hard to fan into a blaze several warm disputes among its inhabitants, of which he happened to become cognizant. At last, however, he was successful, as the progress of our story will show.

CHAPTER 2

As there was not a great deal of money circulating in the neighborhood of Cedardale, the blacksmith, the shoemaker, the joiner, and even the schoolmaster — took grain and other products in return for their labor; so that most of the families resident in and around the village had need of the services of Mr. White, the miller.

One day Nancy Wimble, the shoemaker's wife, had occasion to go to the mill. She could have sent Dick as well; but, as she wanted to have a little gossip with the miller, she preferred going herself. The mill stood nearly a quarter of a mile from Nancy's dwelling; and so, borrowing, as was her custom on like occasions, the blacksmith's old brown horse, she took her bag of grain and departed on her errand.

The miller was grinding a grist when she arrived, and she was obliged, therefore, to wait until he was ready to attend to her. In the meantime, she plied with many questions the boy who had come with this grist, and whose family she knew very well. By these means she succeeded in gaining intelligence from the unsuspecting lad, of several private matters appertaining to the present state of the family. Over these her mind brooded, and she soon *magnified* into importance, mere casual things.

The miller was at last ready to grind her wheat. While the grain was passing from the hopper through the millstones, and thence by "conveyers" and "elevators" to the story above to be bolted, Mr. White, who was himself a little chatty, and quite willing to hear ill-natured things said of his neighbors, had a few words of gossip with Nancy Wimble.

"How is your neighbor Striker and family?" said he. "I see you have his old horse, as usual."

There was something in the miller's tone when he said "as usual" that Nancy did not exactly like. She replied to his question by a peculiar drawing down of her mouth and chin, and an elevation of her eyebrows, at the same time saying coldly —

"So, so — same old two-and-sixpence. And, by the by, Mr. White," added Nancy, in whose ears continued to sound the words 'as usual', "I heard Mrs. Striker saying some rather hard things about you, the other day."

"Of me! Hard things of me! What can *she* have to say of me, I would like to know?"

The miller's face flushed a little, and his voice showed that he was unpleasantly excited.

"Nothing more than the truth, I reckon," replied Nancy, affecting a careless air, and smiling as she spoke.

"Nothing more than the truth! Well, *what* was it? As you have excited my curiosity, the least you can do is to gratify it."

"It's of no consequence," said Nancy, "nothing to be minded. Hannah Striker was always a suspicious kind of body. She wouldn't trust her own father, I believe."

"Wouldn't trust her own father! What has that to do with me?"

"You remember the last bag of wheat you ground for her?" said Nancy, speaking low, and with the air of one who has something of importance to communicate.

"I do, certainly."

"Well — now you mustn't breathe a word of this — well, I happened to be in there a little while after she came back from your mill, and she was weighing the meal and measuring the shorts, and seemed to be all in a pucker about something. 'What's the matter?' said I, 'Is anything wrong?' She didn't make any answer at first, but went on weighing and measuring, until she at last appeared satisfied about something. 'Well, Hannah, what is it?' I now again asked. She took a long, deep breath, looked very important — you know she can look awfully so, when she pleases — and said: 'Something wrong here, Nancy — something wrong, depend on it. This grist doesn't measure out. And, do you know,' she went on to say, 'that there is a good deal of talk about White the miller. People are not satisfied. There's a *screw* loose somewhere, you may be sure.'"

"Grist didn't measure out! Screw loose! What does the hussy mean?" exclaimed the instantly excited miller, fairly sputtering out his words.

"Now don't fly off the handle all at once," said Nancy soothingly; yet inwardly delighted to see the effect of her barbed words.

"Fly off the handle, ha! Tell me that I am called a rogue and a cheat, and then say, 'Don't fly off the handle all at once.' What kind of stuff do you think I'm made of?"

"You're too *touchy*," replied Nancy Wimble, with great composure, "too touchy by far. Besides, who said anything about your being a rogue and a cheat? Not I, certainly."

"But Hannah Striker said that her grist didn't measure out, and that there was a screw loose in my mill."

"Well, if it didn't measure out, it didn't — that's all, neighbor White. And if Hannah's story is true, that there were two bushels and a peck in her bag of wheat, then there is something wrong, for I saw her meal weighed, and there was only eighty pounds."

"And how much would you have, mam?" inquired the miller sharply.

"Hannah says that she was entitled to *ninety* pounds."

"Indeed! Well, how did she figure it out?"

"She says that two bushels and a peck of wheat will make just one hundred pounds of flour."

"Ninety-eight pounds," replied the miller, "always taking it for granted that the wheat weighs sixty pounds — which Hannah Striker's didn't by a great deal."

"The cost, she said, would be just ten pounds in the hundred."

"She's wrong," said the miller. "I won't grind even the parson's grist for less than an eighth. That would have brought her meal from ninety-eight pounds down to eighty-six, even if the wheat had been up to the standard weight, which it was far from being."

This was so plain a statement of the case, that Nancy, who had encouraged the blacksmith's wife in her suspicions against the miller, and even related some of her own experiences and impressions, saw the matter in rather a different light than before. Had she been a right-minded, peace-loving woman, she could have at once extinguished the *little flame* her words had kindled. This, however, she was not. No peacemaker was Nancy Wimble, but a *lover of discord*. So, at once changing her tone and manner, she replied to the miller —

"That's just what I told her; but she was deaf as an adder to all reason."

Liars and busybodies should have good memories. But, it is to be noted that such is rarely the case, nature having provided, seemingly, the *defect* as an *antidote* to the poison that is under their tongues. How few there are, however, who wisely apply the antidote! The miller did not, in this case, although, but a little while back, Nancy had *herself* objected to the eighty pounds as insufficient.

"Just what I told her," repeated Nancy. "I know the wheat very well. They got it from old Gill. We had some of it, and it was a real cheat."

"Something wrong, ha! A screw loose! I'm to be called an old cheat and robber at this time of life, and by Hannah Striker? Better look to her *drunken husband*, and see that he doesn't lame any more of his neighbors' horses, while shoeing them, by driving nails the wrong way."

"So say I. And, by the way, it's my notion that Mary Green ought to make him pay smartly for crippling her mare. The animal won't be good for anything these six months to come. Her hoof, it is said, will come off."

"Six months!" replied the miller. "If in a year, it will be a wonder."

"Striker's going to the dogs fast enough," remarked Nancy. "He's drinking harder than ever. Some months ago, there was a talk of his moving away from Cedardale. I wish in my heart he would go."

"The family's *no credit* to the village, that's certain," said the miller.

"You might say a *disgrace* to the village, and not be much out of the way," insinuated Nancy.

"A disgrace, then, if you will have it so; and, if it comes in your way, you may tell them that I say so. Take too much money, ha! I'll never forgive Hannah Striker for that, as long as I live. Stephen White's honest, and every man, woman, and child knows or ought to know it. Take too much money! How did she think I got it? Didn't she stand by and see me weigh her flour?"

"She thinks, perhaps," replied Nancy, who had an exceedingly fertile imagination, "that there are *two spouts* leading from the millstones; one into the conveyers, and the other into a secret box or bag belonging to the miller."

Stephen White, who was sitting on a bag of grain when Nancy said this, sprang to his feet as suddenly as if there had been an explosion by his side.

"Two spouts! A secret bag! Did Hannah Striker dare to say that?" he cried, almost foaming with rage.

"No — no — don't misunderstand me. I didn't just say that Hannah used *these exact* words."

"Two spouts, indeed! Upon my word!" The miller had taken no heed to the evasive remark of Nancy Wimble. "I'm an old cheat — a robber! But she'll hear of it, she will! A secret box! Isn't it too much for mortal man to bear?"

"Now don't misunderstand me, neighbor White" said Nancy. "I didn't say that Hannah Striker told me that you had two spouts running from the millstones."

"Who did say it, then, I'd like to know?"

"I didn't say that anybody said it."

"You didn't?"

"No."

"Then what did you say?"

"That, *perhaps*, Hannah Striker thought so."

"Bah! Do you think I'm a fool or a dolt? Somebody has got up this lying story," answered the miller, who was not to be soothed by any evasions. "And until I know better, I shall believe it originated with Striker's wife. She's not too good for anything; that's my opinion of her."

"And mine is not the most flattering in the world" remarked Nancy. "Still, I wish you to remember distinctly, that I did not say Hannah *originated* this report."

"If she didn't, you did then," said the excited miller, who had the fault or merit, whichever it might he regarded, of speaking out, sometimes, whether to a person's face or behind his back, just what he thought of him.

"Me!" It was now Nancy's turn to be moved.

"Me, did you say, Stephen White?" and she crossed her arms, and fixed her indignant eyes on the miller's face.

"It lies between you, certainly," was answered, "and one of you will have to acknowledge its authorship, or give me some other authority. Do you think I'm going to rest under such a slander? If so, you are wonderfully mistaken. Stephen White values his good name far too highly. And now, if Hannah Striker actually said that I take, by secret means, more than is just, speak out plainly. I'm bound to know the author. At present, it lies between you and her. You can act as you please."

Nancy Wimble had indulged herself in a spirit of *detraction* and *mischief-making* a little too far; and she was now conscious of this. She tried to make light of the matter; but this wouldn't do. The miller, who was really correct in his dealings, and who loved to be thought an *honest* man, had been touched in too tender a place. If there was such a report about him, he was bound to know its author.

When he and Nancy parted, it was not with very amiable feelings toward each other; as the miller had refused to make light of what she had said, and persisted in asserting that the slander lay between her and the blacksmith's wife.

"What a mean, miserable fellow that Stephen White is," said Nancy Wimble, on going over to Hannah Striker's, for the purpose of returning the old brown horse she had borrowed.

"I always knew that" was Hannah's reply. "Have you weighed your meal?"

"No, I saw the miller weigh it."

"Take my advice, and weigh it yourself. I wouldn't trust his weights."

"He'd hardly have light weights," replied Nancy to this; "it would be so easily detected. Millers can use other and more secret means to double-charge."

"So I have heard. Secret spouts, and the like."

"That's it! — that's it" said Nancy, in a quick voice. "These are not so easily found out."

Hannah did not, in the conversation which followed, assert that miller White had such spouts, hard as Nancy tried to get her to do so. Enough, however, was said to enable Nancy to screen herself by its *exaggeration* and *warped repetition*, if the miller pressed his investigations as was threatened. She was hardly clear in her mind as to the policy of giving Mrs. Striker the benefits of Stephen White's opinion of herself and family, which she had provoked him to express so freely, as strong as was her natural inclination to do so. This inclination, encouraged by the thought that if she could get the miller and the blacksmith's family into a sharp quarrel, she might deflect attention from herself as the first instigator, turned the scale in her mind, and caused her to say —

"One thing is certain, Hannah, White never speaks well of anybody. He seems eaten up with *envy*."

"I've long seen that," replied Mrs. Striker.

"He has a *grudge* against you and your husband!"

"What is the reason?"

"Heaven knows. I reckon he can't find a good word for us in his dictionary."

"No, indeed; I'm sorry to say that he cannot. He speaks very hard of you," replied Nancy.

"He does, ha!" This declaration on the part of Nancy Wimble, at once *fevered the mind* of her auditor.

"I wouldn't have meddled in this matter, for I never like to make trouble between neighbors," said Nancy in a low insinuating voice, and with the air of one who was forcing herself, from *duty*, to serve a friend; "but, indeed, Hannah, it wouldn't be right for me to keep silence, when any one talks about a neighbor, as White talks about you."

"About us! how does he talk about us, please?"

"Well, Hannah, to tell you the honest truth, White says your family is a *disgrace* to the village of Cedardale, and he'll be glad of the day when you all move out of it. There! that's what he said — and my cheek burns to tell you; still, it's the honest truth, and you ought to know it. But isn't it a poison shame that *he*, of all others, should say so!"

Poor Mrs. Striker! With an intemperate husband, and the ever-present consciousness that they were becoming poorer and poorer every day, she carried always a weight upon her feelings. Too well did she understand that allusion was made to her weak, besotted husband, for whom, fallen as he was, there still lingered in her bosom much of the old tenderness. Striker was never ill-natured to her, even in his worst moments. If she talked to him about his habits, when sober, he would acknowledge his fault with strong self-condemnation, and promise amendment. She was never so unwise as to scold or use harsh and cutting words to him when he was in liquor; and so, in her suffering and sorrow, she was spared the heavy consequences that are visited on the heads of, alas! too many wives, who are *cursed* with drunken husbands. There was good in her life-companion, as well as evil; and she had ever tried to look at the good as steadily as possible — a difficult task, we must own.

All the quick anger which Nancy Wimble had at first conjured up, subsided under the mortification and sharp pain from which Mrs. Striker now suffered. Her flushed countenance became gradually pale. Once or twice she tried to speak, but a rising in her throat, warned her that in the attempt she would be overcome by her feelings. At last, in the fullness of her heart, she exclaimed —

"Oh, Nancy! Nancy! this is indeed hard!"

And covering her face with her hands, she wept silently, while the hot tears dropped fast from between her fingers, and fell upon the floor.

The shoemaker's wife was momentarily touched by this unexpected exhibition of feeling, and a passing emotion of regret stirred the surface of her icy heart. Then rising, she bid her weeping neighbor a hurried good day, and returned to her own home, to collect her thoughts, and plan some mode of avoiding any *consequences* to herself that might possibly arise from the quarrel she had so skillfully provided for the two families of the miller and blacksmith.

CHAPTER 3

While Nancy Wimble was revolving in her mind the best mode of escaping the responsibility likely to rest upon her for getting the miller and the blacksmith into a quarrel, *Mary Green* came in to see her husband, with a pair of shoes that required mending. Mary had scarcely darkened the door of Wimble's little workshop, before Nancy, who had seen her pass the window, near which she stood at work, entered also.

"Good day, neighbor Green! How are you? and how are all the children?" inquired Nancy in her animated way.

"Quiet well, I thank you," replied Mrs. Green.

"How's your *horse* Fanny?" pursued Nancy.

The countenance of the visitor fell, at this question, and she replied —

"Bad enough. I'm afraid the poor creature will never he good for anything again."

"Indeed! Why, Mary, this is dreadful!" Nancy's countenance expressed great concern.

"It's very bad, certainly," returned Mrs. Green in a somber voice.

"What does *Striker* say about it?" asked the shoemaker.

"Say? What can he say? He's *crippled* the poor beast, and that is the beginning and the end of it."

"If it were my horse," said the shoemaker, with indignation, "it wouldn't be the end of it, by a great deal. Striker has injured your property — and he should pay for it."

"That he should," chimed in Nancy, "and if I were you, I'd *make* him do it. He was tipsy, of course, when he drove that nail the wrong way. If he will drink — then let him pay for the injury he does when drunk. It's rather hard that a poor widow like you, should have to suffer for his bad doings."

"So I think," replied Mary, who began to feel more distinctly conscious of the great wrong she had sustained, and now quite forgot the offer of the blacksmith to let her have his old brown horse whenever she might want him, so long as her mare was useless from her lame foot. "So I think. But what can a poor lone woman do?"

"There's as good a *law* for you as for anyone else," said the shoemaker.

"Law?" Mary Green hardly comprehended her neighbor Wimble.

"Yes, law. It is made for the poor as well as for the rich. Indeed, I'm of Mr. Sharp's way of thinking — Mr. Sharp, who lives over at Elderglen. He says that the use of law is to protect the weak against the strong — the poor against the rich. The strong man and the rich man can protect themselves — it is only the poor and the weak that need protection."

"That's the right doctrine. I go in for that," spoke out Nancy Wimble, decidedly and with animation. "Yes, indeed! I'd have some kind of *satisfaction* out of Striker, or let him take the consequences. It will be a *good lesson* for him."

"He did offer," said Mrs. Green, now recollecting herself, "to lend me his old brown horse almost any time."

"His old brown horse!" Nancy Wimble spoke with contempt. "Does he think you'd ride his old brown horse, unless it were to the mill, or some such place? I'd like to see you riding to church, or even to Elderglen to visit your sister, on that miserable old rawbone! That was little better than an *insult*."

And so now it really seemed to Mary Green.

"I'll tell you what I would do," said the shoemaker. "I'd go to Striker, and be very plain with him. He's injured your property, and it is no more than right that he should *pay all the damage*. Say to him that while you are not disposed to be hard, you will expect him to make some *reparation* for the loss you have suffered. This is but fair and right; and, if he is an honest man, he will at once agree to pay you something. If he refuses, he is not honest, and should be *made* to do what is right. And be very sure that the *law* will bring him to his bearings mighty quick."

"He ought to pay you at least twenty dollars," remarked Nancy.

"*Twice* twenty," said the shoemaker. "Still, if he will pay you twenty dollars, I would take it, and so save trouble."

"I shall be perfectly satisfied with twenty," replied Mrs. Green, whose real loss in the matter was far from being so serious as her false friends were trying to make her believe. Fanny, the mare, whose hoof had been injured by the blacksmith's carelessness, passed, at any rate, two-thirds of her time in the stable, or roaming about the fields, for her owner rode her but seldom. And now that she was crippled for a season, there were a dozen neighbors from whom she could get a horse, and welcome, quite as often as she wished to ride.

For all this, the *earnest way* in which the shoemaker and his wife commented on the wrong she had suffered, and their positive declaration that she was entitled to, and ought to get damages, made her really believe herself a *seriously injured* woman.

"I'll go and see Striker this very day," said she warmly.

"That I would," urged the shoemaker. And "That I would," chimed in his wife.

Meanwhile, there was quite an exciting time at the blacksmith's. Poor Mrs. Striker still sat weeping, and with her face hidden by her hands, as at the departure of Nancy Wimble, when her husband, having need of some article in the house, came in from his shop. He saw, at a glance, that something was wrong, and said in a kind voice —

"Hannah."

But she neither moved nor made answer.

"Hannah," he repeated; "Hannah, what ails you?"

The only reply to this was a bursting sob, the more violent from a strong effort at repression. For a moment the unhappy woman wept bitterly. Her husband rarely, if ever, became impatient with, or angry toward his much-enduring, long-suffering wife. She had ever been a good wife to him, and well he knew it. And if ever he made resolutions of sobriety, they were prompted by affection for her. Alas! that these resolutions were so very, very weak. Now, he felt no impatience; but was touched by her affliction, and anxious to know the cause. So he sat down by her side, and laying his hand upon her arm, said —

"Hannah, dear, won't you say what is wrong? What makes you cry so?"

"Oh, John," replied the weeping wife, and as she lifted her tearful face, she pressed her hand tightly against her bosom, as if there was pain there, "I felt just now as if my heart would break."

"For what cause, Hannah? What new trouble has come?"

"It is from something I heard a little while ago," was replied.

"Brought by that idle gossip, Nancy Wimble, I suppose," said Striker, with a sudden anger in his voice.

"The words were no less sharp, because they came to my ears from her tongue," answered the wife.

"What did she say?"

"She was just from the mill."

"Yes."

"White, you know, has little good feeling for us."

"Quite as much as we have for him, I reckon. Well, what of Mr. White?"

"Nancy said that he had been speaking very hard of us, and, as a good neighbor, she thought it but right to repeat to me his language."

"What did he say?" The face of Striker had flushed instantly.

"He said that our family was a *disgrace* to Cedardale, and that he would be glad when we moved out of it."

Unexpectedly to Mrs. Striker, there came no burst of indignation from her husband at this announcement. The red anger which had burned on his face gradually gave place to a more pallid hue. Very still and silent he sat for almost a minute. He had withdrawn the hand at first laid tenderly upon the arm of his wife, and now, with his body erect, and his eyes fixed in thought, he seemed pondering deeply some newly-suggested question or purpose. At length, with a heavy sigh, he answered in a subdued voice —

"He had no cause to say this of you, Hannah. None in the world. O dear! I wish I had — "

What was in the mind of the blacksmith became no further apparent; for, rising up suddenly, he left the room and returned to his shop, where he resumed his work. He had stood by the anvil only a short time, when he laid down his hammer, and going to an old barrel in a corner of the shop, took therefrom a small flask of liquor, and was about raising it to his lips, when a thought flashing through his mind produced a pause. Slowly the hand which held the bottle receded from its elevated position. He stood musing and irresolute for some moments — sighed deeply — muttered some incoherent words between his teeth — then replaced the flask in the barrel, without having tasted its contents, and went back to his work.

There were *better purposes* in the mind of the blacksmith. He felt the *shame* his bad habits had brought upon his family; and his mind was struggling in the formation of *good resolutions* for the future. Alas! that these were so quickly to be scattered.

So soon as White, the miller, could make arrangements to leave his mill, off he started, boiling over with resentment, to see Mr. Striker about the *slanders* which his wife had been putting in circulation to his injury.

"Look here, Striker!" said he, on entering the old shanty where the blacksmith was sweating over his anvil, "I've got a crow to pick with you."

"Have you, indeed," was the blacksmith's answer, as he let his hammer rest on the block, and straightened himself up. The two men looked, each with contracting brow, into each other's face, for some moments.

"That busy-tongued wife of yours!" began the excited miller.

White saw, by the scowl of anger that instantly darkened the face of his neighbor, that the few words already spoken were likely to arouse the blacksmith's temper to a pitch beyond what he had calculated upon, and therefore checked the further utterance that was on his lips.

"If you don't leave my shop this instant, I'll throw you out, neck and heels!" cried Striker, the moment he found utterance.

The miller, at this unexpected retort, staggered back a pace or two in surprise and alarm. There was *murder* in the eyes of the blacksmith, and he saw it. What the end would have been, we know not, but, at that moment, a man rode up to the door of the smithy, and, dismounting, asked to have his horse shod. White, taking advantage of this, immediately retired — not, however, in a spirit of self-reproof for having spoken so roughly to the blacksmith, but full of *anger* against his neighbor.

"Pleasant village, this," remarked the stranger, as Striker took up the horse's foot, and began to prepare it for a new shoe.

"It may be to some. I've never found it so very pleasant," was the blacksmith's answer, made in a repellant tone.

"There's not a pleasanter village within fifty miles," continued the stranger, not appearing to notice the crusty mood of the smith.

"Glad you think so," answered Striker, his voice in no way modified.

"What's the matter, my friend?" asked the man, in a cheerful, good-natured voice. "Something must be wrong, or you would never answer a stranger's civil remark after this fashion."

"You want your horse shod, don't you?" Striker raised himself up, and looked with a scowling face at his customer as he asked this question.

"Oh, certainly. I've said as much already. What else could have brought me here?"

"Very well; be content with that!" sharply replied the smith.

Over the mild, benevolent face of the stranger, a middle-aged man, in the dress of a farmer, there passed a slight shadow. He did not seem either hurt or offended at the blacksmith's rudeness; but rather *grieved* to see him in such an unhappy state.

"Take care, my friend," said he, as he stood looking on while the smith was driving the nails into the horse's hoof, "I had a fine animal injured not long ago by a nail accidentally turned the wrong way."

Now this was *touching a sore place*; for, since the accident to Mary Green's mare, Striker had been annoyed a great deal by remarks upon his carelessness from one and another — not made in an over-kind spirit — and, in his present confusion of mind, it seemed that the stranger knew of this, and had made his last remark on purpose to *wound* him.

The horse's foot dropped instantly to the ground. With erect body, and eyes flashing fire, the smith said fiercely —

"If you're *afraid* to have me shoe your horse, why did you bring him to me?"

"My good friend," said the farmer, in kind and soothing tones, "you seem to be in a strange mood today. The fact of having a horse injured in the way suggested, naturally enough makes me a little fearful, and causes me to utter a *word of caution*, almost involuntarily, whenever I see a blacksmith attempt to drive a nail. I can assure you that I meant no reflection on *your* skill whatever."

Striker muttered, in ill-natured tones, an incoherent reply, and then resumed his work.

The stranger deemed it wisest to make no further remark, and so remained silent, but observant, until the shoeing was completed. Then he paid the price asked for the service, mounted his horse, and rode off.

Scarcely had he left the shop, before Striker went to the *barrel* from which he had previously taken the flask of liquor, and did not turn from it until after drinking a deep draught of the *fiery poison*.

Meantime the stranger took his way toward the *mill*, whose great wheel he had seen slowly revolving in the distance. He found the miller in scarcely a better state of mind than the blacksmith — though with this difference — while the latter was blind and insolent in his ill-nature, the former was polite to his interrogator, but passionate in his denunciation of the blacksmith, whom he represented as the *worst man in the village*. "You may be thankful," said he, in conclusion, "that he hasn't crippled your horse for life."

Next the stranger stopped at the shoemaker's. Here he was treated with a running commentary upon all the leading personages of Cedardale; but he heard not of the existence of a single virtue in any one of them. The *worst* things were said of the miller and the blacksmith.

"Rather poor encouragement to settle in this neighborhood," said he. "What a pity that, where God has made all so perfect — that there should be no moral beauty."

And he rode thoughtfully away from Cedardale.

CHAPTER 4

Scarcely had the excited blacksmith replaced his flask of liquor, from which he had taken a deep draught, in its secret repository, before another visitor entered his shop. It was *Mary Green*. She had come, instigated by the Wimbles, to demand some kind of *remuneration* for the injury she had sustained.

"Good day, Mr. Striker," said she. There was an expression on her face, that the blacksmith did not at all like.

"Good day, Mary," he simply responded; and then awaited the further will of his visitor. Of this he was not long in doubt.

"I've come to have some talk with you about *Fanny*," said she.

"Well — what about her?" returned Striker. "How is she getting along?"

"She'll lose her hoof, of course, and be of no use to me or anybody else, for the next six months or more."

"I'm sorry. But what can I do?" replied the blacksmith. "The foot is wounded, and there is now no help for it. I've already told you that my old brown horse is at your service, whenever you want him; be it on week-day or Sunday. What more can you ask?"

"Old brown horse!" Mary Green spoke with a strong expression of contempt.

"Why do you speak and look so, Mary Green?" said the blacksmith, contracting his heavy brows, and exhibiting many signs of the impatience he felt.

She did not utter the disparaging words about "old sorrel" that were rising to her tongue, but merely said —

"All very well — and I'm obliged for the offer. But that doesn't *mend* Fanny's foot. Besides, I'm used to Fanny, and don't like to ride any other animal."

"Do you think I can mend the beast's foot? ha?" The blacksmith was becoming more and more *fretted* every moment. "Do you want an *iron* hoof? If so, bring her along, and I'll put one on."

The last sentence was uttered in a *sneering* tone, and *chafed* Mary Green a good deal.

"There's one thing you *can* do," said she, "and one thing you *ought* to do — I'm a poor widow, and you have injured my property."

"What *ought* I to do, ha?"

"I wonder that you can ask," said Mary Green. "Everybody says you should do it."

"Do what?" asked the blacksmith.

"Why, *pay damages.*"

"Damages?" echoed the blacksmith.

"Certainly. Everybody in Cedardale says you ought to pay me at least twenty dollars for *crippling* Fanny."

"Twenty dollars!" Striker was made angry at this, beyond all control. "Twenty dollars!" he repeated, and then added passionately, "Just take yourself away from here in double-quick time! Twenty dollars for the hoof of a miserable, old, bleary-eyed, shambling beast that never was worth half the money! Do you think I'm a fool?"

"I think you were *drunk* when you lamed Fanny," retorted Mrs. Green, now quite as angry as the blacksmith. "And if I don't make you pay well for it, there's no law in the land."

"Drunk! Law! Mary Green! This from you?"

The fire grew suddenly dim in the blacksmith's eyes, and his voice, which before was harsh and resentful, became lower in tone and shorn of its steadiness. But Mary Green, now blind from passion, perceiving not this change, sharply answered —

"Yes, drunk! You shall have law to your heart's content. Call my Fanny a miserable, old, bleary-eyed, shambling beast, ha! as if it wasn't enough in you to lame her for life. Oh! but you shall *pay* for this. I'll have remuneration, if there is law or justice in the land — I will!"

Irritated — yet deeply hurt by the words of Mary Green — words so unexpected, as coming from her lips — Striker felt himself again losing his self-control. He did not wish at that time to use any more harsh or cutting words, and so, taking her by the arm, he led her, with some force, to the door of his shop, and pushing her out, said, with more sadness than anger in his voice —

"Go now, Mary Green — go! I didn't expect this from *you.*"

"And what did you expect, ha?" answered fiercely the now terribly-excited woman, almost *screaming* as she wheeled herself around, and took a defiant attitude right in front of the smithy door. "What did you expect? To cripple my poor Fanny for life; and then *insult* me when I called to ask for remuneration. A nice neighbor you are, indeed! A nice neighbor! But I'll bring you to your feelings — I will. I'll make it cost you a pretty penny before I'm done with you. A miserable, old, bleary-eyed beast, ha! Oh! you shall smart for it!"

And shaking her fist at the half-stupefied blacksmith, Mary Green turned away, and strode off with the firm, rapid steps of a man.

It was astonishing how passion and antagonism had metamorphosed this woman, ordinarily the mildest and least resentful of any of the ill-assorted denizens of Cedardale. Poor Striker, who felt as if suddenly beset by all the malignant influences around him, was absolutely confounded by an *assault* from a quarter so unexpected. For a little while after her disappearance, he stood leaning on the handle of his hammer, in a kind of musing stupor. Then he went again to his liquor-flask, and this time drained its contents to the bottom. Alas! How were all the *good resolutions* that, a little while before, commenced forming themselves in his mind, scattered to the winds. The *grief* of his wife had touched him deeply; and, abjuring in his heart the *fiery poison* which had worked such ruin to them all, he had resolved to become a sober man. And there is no telling how quickly this good resolution, like a seed in the earth, would have struck down its first slender shoots and gathered nutriment and strength — had not the miller and Mary Green, like *evil birds*, picked out the good seed before it had time to germinate.

The entire contents of the blacksmith's flask of liquor, taken within so short a time, proved to be more than he could bear, unaffected as he was, from long habit, by ordinary intoxicating influences. After drinking this second time, he sat down on the edge of his forge, and tried to think over, with some degree of coherence, the exciting events of the last half-hour. But the more he tried to think, the more *confused* became his mind. At length, wearied with thinking and stupefied by liquor, he leaned over, and reclined upon his arm. Thus he remained for a short time. Then bending his arm backward, and behind his head, so as to make of it a sort of pillow, he sank down among the coals and cinders, with his head but a few inches from the smouldering blast on the forge.

Half an hour after nightfall, when his unhappy wife, wearied out with waiting for his return, and anxious on account of his unusual absence, sought for him in his shop, she found him, as he had thus laid himself down, asleep and insensible.

Poor drunkard's wife! We will not attempt to picture the anguish of your breaking heart. A little while ago, there was a *star of hope* in your sky, shining out from amid the rifted cloud — now, alas! all is again darkness and despair!

CHAPTER 5

Thoughtfully the stranger, mentioned in a preceding chapter, rode away from Cedardale. On first gaining one of the hills that overlooked the little cluster of houses which lay so cozily in the valley below, he could not repress an exclamation of pleasure, so impressed was he with the *harmony* and *beauty* of the picturesque, yet quiet landscape.

How harshly jarred the ill-natured words of the crusty blacksmith upon this state of feeling; and quite as harshly jarred the words of the miller and the shoemaker. No wonder that he had murmured to himself, as he rode away, "What a pity that, where God has made all so perfect — there should be *no moral beauty!*"

Musing upon all that he had seen and heard, and half wondering at the strange lack of harmony between the visible things of nature and the hearts of the people, the stranger left the more thickly populated portions of the village. As he moved along, gradually ascending to the higher ground, and getting each moment a broader and more attractive view of the surrounding country, the charm of the scenery again impressed him vividly. He had checked his horse, and was letting his eyes range along the silvery course of the stream which wound through the lovely valley, when suddenly there came sharp, angry words to his ears. He looked around, and saw, under the shade of a large sycamore, three boys, who were quarreling — or, to speak more accurately, two of them were quarreling, while the third was endeavoring to bring the disputants to blows.

The stranger on seeing this instantly dismounted, and after throwing the reins of his horse over a post, leaped the fence that separated the road from the field in which were the young wranglers, and quickly stood among them. He said nothing at first, and the boys, scarcely regarding his presence, showed no inclination to break off their quarrel. Two of them stood, each with a foot advanced until toe nearly touched toe, facing each other showing their teeth, and scowling most bitter defiance.

"Hit me, if you dare, Bill Striker!" said one.
"I dare you to strike first Ben White!" retorted the other.
"You're a coward!"

"You're afraid!"

And such-like words were rapidly thrown backward and forward, while the third member of the trio, who was none other than *Dick Wimble*, the shoemaker's son, tried his best to induce one or the other to begin the combat. At last, fearful that neither Bill Striker nor Ben White would pluck up sufficient courage to give the first blow, he took a chip, and placing it on the head of the former, said —

"Now, Bill, dare him to knock it off; and if he does, give it to him between the two eyes."

"Knock it off, if you dare!" instantly cried Bill Striker. "I dare you to knock it off," he added quickly, bending his head forward to provoke his antagonist.

"He's afraid!" said Dick Wimble.

"Am I?" retorted Ben White, stung by this; and raising his hand, he would have swept the chip from its position, had not the stranger, with timely prudence, reached over and gently lifted the piece of wood from Bill Striker's head.

"What did you do that for?" exclaimed the lad fiercely.

"You can strike me, if you choose," said the man, in a firm, yet mild voice; "but if you do, I will not strike you back again."

His words and manner made an instant impression on the young belligerents. They looked at him curiously, then at each other, and then cast their eyes upon the ground.

"There is some trouble here, of course — some misunderstanding — but no cause for fighting," said the stranger. "In fact, there's *never* any cause for fighting, where people mean right and try to *understand* each other. Now, as I always think it time well spent to try and make up quarrels among both young and old, I'd like to have a little talk with you, and see if a better state of things can't be brought about. Come! here's an old log, suppose we all sit down."

All this, from a stranger, was so different from what these lads had been used to, that they were not only surprised, but a good deal softened in their feelings. The usual way with most of the grown-up denizens of Cedardale, in an affair of this kind, was to threaten a flogging, or to stand by and see the difficulty settled by force of *fists*.

"Come now, here's a seat all ready; and I hardly think we need fear interruption," continued the stranger.

Influenced by a moral power which they neither understood nor felt inclined to resist, the three boys seated themselves on the log, while their *mentor* took his place immediately in front of them on the stump of a fallen tree.

"Your name, I believe, is Bill Striker," said he, looking one of the lads in the face.

"Yes, sir," replied the boy, wondering at the same time within himself how the man, whom he had never seen in all his life, should know his name. He did not remember that, in the excitement of the late quarrel, both his own and his antagonist's name were frequently repeated.

"Does your father live in Cedardale?" was next inquired.

"Yes, sir," briefly answered the boy, as before.

"What business does he follow?"

"He's a blacksmith."

"Ah, indeed, he's the blacksmith?"

"Yes, sir."

"And your name is Ben White?" now speaking to one of the other lads.

Ben gave a nod of his head in token of affirmation.

"And what is your father's business?"

"He's the miller."

"The miller?"

"Yes, sir."

"You can see the mill away off there," spoke up Dick Wimble, with some animation, pointing down the valley.

"I don't think I heard your name," said the stranger, speaking now to Dick.

"His name's Dick Wimble. His father's a shoemaker." This information was volunteered by young Striker.

"Ah, yes. Now I understand. You three boys are the sons of the miller, the blacksmith, and the shoemaker. But it seems to me rather strange that the sons of three men who naturally owe so much goodwill to each other, should get up a quarrel among themselves. What would the miller and the blacksmith do — if it were not for the shoemaker? And what, I wonder, would the shoemaker and blacksmith do — if the miller did not grind their wheat and rye and corn? They ought, therefore, to be fast friends; and the same kind feelings should exist between their children. Don't you think so, my little lad?" addressing Striker.

Bill Striker hung his head, looked, as they say, sheepish, and made no answer.

"What do you say, William White?"

"I don't know," mumbled out the miller's son, his glance also tending downward.

"I'm almost afraid you won't agree with me," said the stranger, looking steadily at Dick Wimble; for, now I remember that you were doing all in your power to set your two young friends to fighting, as if they were no better than *dogs*. And this reminds me that I haven't yet inquired as to the cause of this sad affair. What was the trouble, friend Striker? Suppose you enlighten me?"

But Striker held down his head, and made no reply.

"What do *you* say?" The miller's son was now addressed, and his immediate reply was —

"Bill Striker said I robbed his hen's nest; and I didn't. I'm not a thief." He spoke in a tone of indignation.

"How about this, Striker? Had you good reason for making so serious a charge as that of stealing?" The stranger looked very grave.

"*Somebody* robbed my nest," said Bill, doggedly.

"That may be; but before accusing anyone, you should be very certain. What reason had you for suspecting Ben White?"

"I asked Dick Wimble if he knew, and he said he did."

"Ah!" The stranger turned a penetrating glance upon the shoemaker's son, whose eyes drooped, and whose face became slightly flushed.

"And did he say whom he believed it to be?" further inquired the stranger.

"Yes, sir. He said it was Ben White; and that he saw him go to the nest."

"He's a liar!" spoke out sharply and quickly the miller's son, clenching his fists, and looking angry defiance at Dick Wimble.

"Gently — gently, my lad," said the stranger, soothingly. "Fighting never yet mended an injured reputation. If you are innocent, all will in the end be made clear, and the blame fall, where it ought to rest, upon the *false accuser*. Let us inquire more particularly into this matter. You say, Dick Wimble, that you saw White go to the nest of Striker?"

The shoemaker's son, on whose face the now keen eyes of his interrogator were fixed, looked, in a confused manner, first to the one side and then to the other, but did not reply immediately.

"Come, my lad, speak up." There was now an air of authority about the stranger. "Did you see Ben White go to Bill Striker's hen's nest?"

"I saw him in the woods just back of Mr. Striker's blacksmith-shop; and I — I — *thought* he'd been to the hen's nest."

"Is the hen's nest in the woods just back of the blacksmith's shop?" asked the man, looking steadily at Dick.

"Yes, sir."

"And you thought that Ben had been to rob this nest?"

"Yes, sir."

"It's a lie!" ejaculated the miller's son indignantly.

"There — there" said the stranger mildly; "don't give way to passion. Angry words and hard names do no good."

"Well, it is a lie," persisted White; "and he knows it. I haven't been in the woods back of the blacksmith shop in a week."

"Whereabouts in this woods, is the hen's nest of Bill Striker?" asked the man, addressing Dick Wimble.

"Right down by the old poplar, just in back of the shop," replied Dick promptly.

"He knows so well, I wouldn't wonder if he'd robbed it himself," said Ben White. "I'm sure I never knew before where it was."

Dick was hardly prepared for this sudden shifting of the accusation of theft to himself. All eyes were fixed upon him, and the stranger, as well as his two companions, felt at once, from the change in the boy's manner, that *he* was the real culprit.

"What is that?" asked the man, glancing down at Dick's trousers, where a very striking protuberance was seen in the neighborhood of the pocket.

"Nothing — nothing," answered Dick, now manifesting a good deal of confusion, and placing, as he spoke, his hand over his pocket so as to hide the protuberance which had attracted attention.

"If there is nothing in your pocket, you will not, of course, have any objection to my searching it;" and, as he spoke, the man attempted to put his hand in Dick's pocket. This, however, the boy resisted. A slight struggle ensued, in which something in the pocket was crushed. Further effort at concealment being vain, Dick removed from his trowser's pocket two broken eggs, which the moment Bill Striker saw, he pronounced to have been taken from his hen's nest. All the eggs of his hen were speckled in a peculiar manner, and were hardly to be mistaken.

If further proof were lacking, it was to be found in the guilty face of the boy.

"And so," said the stranger severely, "you, Dick Wimble, are the real culprit in this matter. Was it not enough for you to *rob* the nest of Bill Striker, and then to *falsely accuse* Ben White of the crime — but you must, in the wickedness of your heart, do all in your power to set them fighting like two dogs? Oh, shame! shame! I did not believe there was a boy so evilly inclined as this!"

Then addressing the other two lads, he continued, in a milder voice:

"My dear boys, I hope this will prove a lesson to you, and one not soon forgotten. If I had not happened to come along just now, you would, instigated by this wicked companion, have beaten and torn each other, while there really existed no cause for a quarrel. Are you not sorry, Bill Striker, for having accused Ben White of robbing your nest?"

"Indeed I am, sir," promptly replied the boy. "He was innocent, and I now take back all I said."

"And what do you say, Ben?" The stranger now addressed young White.

"All is forgiven; and here is my hand to it," as promptly responded Ben, extending his hand as he spoke, which was warmly taken by the other.

"But I'll not forgive Dick Wimble," said he, compressing his lips and looking threateningly towards the shoemaker's son, who, in evident fear of consequences likely to be visited on his head, was already moving away.

"Nor I neither," added Bill Striker. "If he doesn't feel the weight of these sledge-hammers" — doubling up his fists, "I'm mistaken."

"Come, come, my lads, all this is wrong again," said the stranger; "and *two wrongs never made a right.* Dick is punished enough already; so, let what he has received suffice. And, in my opinion, he is more the object of your *pity,* than your *anger.* The wicked are never happy. They not only trouble others, but trouble themselves; and, as a general thing, are the greatest sufferers. They can only do occasional wrong to others; but they ever bear about them a dissatisfied, uneasy feeling, and often the severest pains of regret or mortification. No — no; seek not to be revenged on this unhappy boy, for that will be to act from the *same evil influences* which govern him. But rather seek to reclaim him from his evil ways."

"It'll be a hard matter to *reclaim* Dick Wimble," replied the miller's son, smiling to himself at so novel a thought. "Why, everybody says he's the worst boy in Cedardale."

"Evil communications seem, then, to have corrupted good manners," said the stranger to this, "if I am to judge from what I saw a little while ago."

The lads understood this without explanation, and showed by their countenances that they felt the rebuke.

The stranger, who had until now remained seated on the stump of a tree, arose.

"I have now spent considerable time with you," said he, "and as I have some distance to ride, I must be going. I shall, in all probability, be passing through Cedardale again before a great while; and if this should happen, I will certainly look you up and learn whether you have profited any by the good advice now given. Before we part, there is one promise that I wish you both to make."

The boys looked at the man curiously.

"Will you promise?"

Both the lads hesitated.

"Do you think I would ask you to do anything *wrong*?"

"No, sir," was the prompt reply of each.

"I am sure I would not. *If you can do no good — then do no harm,* that is my motto. And it is a very good one. Well, which of you is willing to make me a promise?"

"I will," said Bill Striker, forcing out the words in a way that showed some effort on his part.

"I don't care! So will I," broke in Ben White.

"Very well. That's bravely done. You know that I won't ask you anything wrong; and this willingness to promise, I take as an indication that you would like to do right. Now, all I have to ask is, that you would consider Dick Wimble as sufficiently punished for his fault, and promise not to say a single word to him either about robbing the hen's nest, or making against one of you, a false accusation of theft. Take my word for it, this will be best in the end. Will you promise?"

"I will," promptly answered Ben White; and "I will" came as freely from the lips of Bill Striker.

"Bravely done," returned the stranger encouragingly, as he laid a hand upon each boy's head. "You will be better, wiser, and happier for this. In a week or two, I hope to be in this neighborhood again, when, as before said, I will be sure to see you. So good-by now."

And he shook their hands warmly. Then turning away, he remounted his horse, and rode off, without once looking behind.

The two boys stood silently gazing after this strange man until he had passed entirely out of sight. Then they turned, and looked for some moments into each other's faces.

"I wonder who he is?" said Ben White, speaking after a long breath and in a subdued tone of voice.

"I don't know who he is; but I know one thing," replied his companion.

"What is that?"

"He's the right kind of man."

"So say I. And what's more, I'm going to keep my promise; though I would just like to get my two sledge-hammers on that rascal, Dick Wimble."

"And wouldn't I?" rejoined Striker. "But a promise is a promise, and I'm not going to break my word."

In this spirit the two boys took their way slowly homeward.

CHAPTER 6

Almost blind with passion was Mary Green, as she strode away from the shop of Striker.

"A miserable, old, bleary-eyed, shambling beast!" she muttered, indignantly, at every few paces. "Oh! but he shall *pay* for this!"

As Nancy Wimble's cottage lay in the direct line of her journey homeward, Mary, as well from opportunity as inclination, turned aside to relate her adventure with the blacksmith. It needed but a single glance at her flushed, excited face, to tell Nancy that she had met with a strong rebuff; and, to encourage the freest communication, she said, without waiting for a word from her visitor —

"And so Striker hasn't given you any compensation?"

"Compensation!" exclaimed Mary. "Compensation, indeed! He has *insulted* me in the most outrageous manner!"

"You don't say so!" Nancy Wimble lifted eyes and eyebrows with an expression of the most profound astonishment.

"Yes, I do say. Now, what do you think he called my poor Fanny?"

"I'm sure I cannot tell."

"A miserable, old, good-for-nothing, bleary-eyed, shambling beast!"

"Mary Green!"

"And this isn't all, Nancy. Oh! I can't tell you how he abused me, up and down. And then, would you believe it, he caught hold of my arm with his great dirty hands, and pushed me out of his shop!"

"Oh, Mary Green!"

"It's the truth, Nancy; and my arm is black and blue now, where he seized hold of me."

"Dreadful! dreadful! It's a wonder he hadn't *killed* you."

"A thousand wonders," replied Mrs. Green. "I'm too thankful that I got away without some of my limbs being broken."

"You have cause to be," said Nancy. "But what are you going to do?"

"I'm going to make him smart for it; that's what I'm going to do," was Mary Green's emphatic response.

"You'll not be true to yourself if you don't, that's all I have to say in the matter. Why, if he's allowed to go on in this way, there'll be no living in the village with him. If I was you, Mary, I'd go over to

Elderglen, and see *Mr. Sharp*, the *lawyer*, at once. He'll bring him to his feelings mighty quick."

"Just what I'm going to do!"

At this moment a man alighted from a horse, and after fastening him to a post that stood in front of the door, entered the little shop where Wimble sat busy over his hammer, awl, and lapstone.

"Who's that, I wonder?" said Nancy, going instantly to the window.

Mary Green moved up to her side; but neither of them could make out the visitor.

"I think I've seen him before," said the latter; "but where and when, I cannot for my life tell."

"Wait until he goes away, and then we'll find out all about him."

But the man stayed so long that Mrs. Green became impatient to get home, and took her departure first; not, however before receiving from the shoemaker's wife the strongest repeated injunctions to go over to Elderglen, and get Sharp to bring a suit for damages against Striker.

The man who had called to see Wimble was none other than Sharp himself, as Nancy ascertained immediately on the departure of her visitor; for she then made an errand into her husband's shop, and was introduced to the lawyer.

"Oh, if I'd only known it was you," she said, the moment she understood that the visitor, or customer, as he wished to be considered, was Sharp. "Mary Green was here." The last sentence was addressed to her husband.

"Indeed!" responded the shoemaker. "Did she see Striker?"

"Oh yes! and the way he abused her was shocking." How the lawyer's eyes did brighten!

"Abused her! It isn't possible!" said Wimble.

"It is possible, though, and what is more — she says he caught hold of her, and pushed her out of his shop, bruising her arm most dreadfully."

"Assault and battery!" said Sharp.

"And what do you think it was all for?" asked the shoemaker, addressing the lawyer. "I'll tell you. He drove a nail the wrong way in shoeing Mary Green's mare, crippling the poor beast, it may be, for life; and Mary just went over to talk to him about it."

"She can make him pay for it," said the lawyer.

"So I told her."

"And what is more," spoke up Nancy, "she's going to make him do it. She wants to see you, Mr. Sharp, particularly; and, if you'll call at her house on your way home, you'll save her trouble, and do her a great favor into the bargain."

"Does she live in the little white cottage just at the foot of Beech Hill?" remarked the lawyer.

"Yes; that's her house. You'll call, won't you, as you go home?" urged Nancy.

"If I thought she really wished to see me, I'd call, certainly," said Sharp, affecting modesty and indifference.

"Well, she does want to see you, I can tell you that. It's a good way for her to walk over to Elderglen, and her mare is a cripple," said Nancy.

"I'll think about it," returned Sharp.

Soon after, he took his departure, and was at Mary Green's cottage almost as early as the excited widow herself. On mentioning his name, he met with a cordial reception, and found a client ready for his able services. Two suits were proposed, one for *damages* sustained in consequence of the injury to Fanny's foot; the other for *assault and battery*; and the lawyer was formally instructed to commence proceedings immediately. When he left the cottage of Mary Green, and took his way toward Elderglen, he had five dollars more in his pocketbook than was there when he entered — and the widow's purse was lighter by precisely that amount.

The night that followed the closing of this day, brought with it even greater disquietude than usual to the leading personages in Cedardale; for the shoemaker and his wife had managed to *fan the fire of discord* into a flame that burned with unusual fierceness. The saddest heart in the village was that of Mrs. Striker. A gleam of hope had shot suddenly across her heart; but how quick had all become even darker than before. She had looked for her husband's return at close of day with trembling interest. Alas! how her heart died within her as the darkness fell, and he remained absent to an unusual time. More than confirmed, at last, were all her worst fears, when she found him stupefied with drink, and asleep on his forge.

Yet, amid her grief and pain, there came one little ray of comfort to the heart of Mrs. Striker, the more grateful that it was so altogether unlooked for. Her eldest son, William, of whom the reader already knows something, was, we are sorry to say, a very bad and troublesome boy, whose appearance at home was generally the signal for discord. His father had little or no control over him, because he was despised on account of his intemperance; and he had not sufficient love for his mother to lead him to act in any obedience to her wishes. He followed therefore, mainly, the promptings of his own perverse inclinations. To the younger children, he had become a terror.

It was after sundown when the lad returned home. His little brother and sister were playing on the floor as he entered the house, and were in some trouble about a wooden horse which they in vain tried to harness to their wagon.

"Now don't touch it, Bill," cried one of the children, the moment they saw their brother; and each of them showed signs of fear, lest he should, as usual, either kick the playthings across the room, or appropriate them entirely to his own amusement.

The boy, however, showed no inclination to trouble them, but sat down quietly by a window, and, leaning his head upon his hand, appeared lost in thought. His mother noticed this unusual occurrence with some surprise.

For four or five minutes, the two children on the floor tried, but in vain, to adjust the harness of their wooden horse — their failure marked, every now and then, by angry or impatient exclamations. Attracted, at length, by their voices, the elder brother observed their efforts for some moments, and then said, with an unexpected kindness of manner —

"If you'll let me, I'll fix it for you."

"No you won't; you'll break it all in pieces," replied one of the children.

"I'll fix it all right, if you'll let me," said the lad, now rising and approaching the children.

The real interest and kindness in his tones were so apparent, that the two little ones permitted him to do for them as he proposed. In a few moments the horse was rightly harnessed to the wagon, and the children were drawing them about the floor with glad voices and countenances beaming with pleasure. William resumed his seat, and regarded them with looks of satisfaction.

"It was *kind* of you, William," said Mrs. Striker. The boy glanced up into his mother's face, and she could not help remarking a gentleness, and even beauty of expression, once so often visible on his countenance, yet faded, she had long since feared, forever.

Darkness came at length, and what was unusual, Mr. Striker had not yet returned to his family.

"How long your father stays out!" remarked Mrs. Striker, coming into the house, after having stood for some time at the door, straining her eyes into the dusky atmosphere, in the hope of seeing her husband's approaching form. "Come, William," she added, "won't you go with me over to the shop, and see what it is that keeps him away so long?"

But for the change in the boy's state of mind just manifested, Mrs. Striker would not have made this request. And even now she partly held her breath, in suspense, for the answer, lest it should be, as of old, an ill-natured rejection of her wishes. But, instead of this, the boy started to his feet in prompt obedience, saying as he did so —

"Yes, mother," in a voice so cheerful that it caused the heart of Mrs. Striker, even under the heavy weight which lay upon it, to bound upward with a pleasant emotion.

Their visit to the smithy resulted in finding the one they sought, sleeping heavily in a drunken slumber, upon the forge, from which the smouldering fires had long since gone out. After much trouble the husband and father was aroused to a semi-consciousness, and, supported on one side by his wife, and on the other by his son, led away to his home. On being taken into the room where he slept, he sank down upon the bed; and was, in a few moments, as entirely lost to external things as before his removal from the smithy.

By the side of the bed sat down poor Mrs. Striker, and sobbed aloud in the uncontrollable bitterness of her hopeless sorrow; and near her bent her son, weeping too, and deeply touched by his mother's grief. The mother soon perceived that her boy wept also — perceived it with surprise and something of a strange gladness — if such a word may be used for such a feeling.

Thus, amid her grief and pain, there came a little ray of comfort; and in it her heart recognized, tremblingly, the promise of a new light that would make less dismal, the darkness of her unhappy lot.

CHAPTER 7

The week that followed the events already described, was one of no little excitement in Cedardale. Trouble was rife on every hand.

The morning that followed to the day on which Mary Green had demanded of Striker, the blacksmith, the payment of damages for injury done to her mare, found the latter sober in every sense of the word — sober in mind as well as body. He remembered distinctly the visits of both White the miller, and Mrs. Green; and the effect upon himself, in driving him to the bottle, which he had resolved, once more, to abandon. The sad eyes of his wife, that were occasionally bent on him in pleading silence, but too well assured him of the debasing results which had followed this speedy abandonment of a good resolution.

"Poor, miserable wretch!" Thus he sighed to himself; and as he sighed, he turned his face to the wall; and tightly closing his eyelids, sought vainly to expel from his mind a crowd of upbraiding images.

This sigh, and this sudden movement, did not escape the attention of his wife, who had already arisen, and was busying herself about the room in various household duties. She came at once to the bedside, and leaning over, said in a sad, yet tender voice —

"John."

The blacksmith made no answer.

"John," she repeated, with even increased tenderness in her voice.

A deep sigh — almost a groan — was the husband's only response.

"All may yet be well, John." How earnestly, affectionately, and encouragingly was this said! Almost heart-broken and discouraged, it was astonishing how the poor woman schooled her voice. She was, at heart, a true woman, or she could never have accomplished the task.

"Oh, Hannah! Don't speak to me so!" replied Striker, his tones betraying deep emotion. He did not move, nor turn his face from the wall.

"It is the truth, John," said his wife, encouragingly. "Haven't I always said it?"

The response to this was another long-drawn sigh.

"I have always said it, and I will hope on to the end," continued Mrs. Striker. "There were pleasant days for us in the past, John — very pleasant; and I cannot give up the hope of days to come as full of pleasantness."

"Hannah! Hannah!" Striker now turned his face to his wife, and she saw that it was almost distorted by struggling emotions. "May God sustain your hope — there is no strength in me! Yesterday, I vowed, in all sincerity, that I would be a changed man. But, oh, how quickly did I fail!"

"Why, why did you touch it, John?" answered his wife, her manner changing to one of great earnestness. "You are a free man."

"Ah, Hannah! You do not know how I was tempted. I had scarcely reached my shop, yesterday, after leaving you, when in came *White*. My blood boiled the moment I saw him. Knowing how scandalously he had talked about us, I could scarcely refrain from ordering him off the moment I set eyes on him. Before I could speak, he said in the most insolent manner — 'Look here! I've got a crow to pick with you!' — and then made some reference to you as a 'busy-tongued woman.' I couldn't stand this, no how; and if he hadn't gone off mighty quick, I'd have pitched him into the road, neck and heels. Oh! I was terrible angry. In this state, all my good resolutions were forgotten, and I drank again."

"What had I done? What did he mean by calling me a busy-tongued woman?" asked Mrs. Striker, with a flushing face and trembling voice.

"Heaven knows! I gave him no time for explanation. I was too angry. But it is some of *Nancy Wimble's* work, no doubt. A dog that will fetch a bone — will carry one, you know. She had a long rigmarole to tell of White's abuse of us; and, no doubt, she had as much to say on the other side."

"But what *could* she say, John?"

"Liars and busybodies are never much at a loss, you know. Something, dropped from your lips in unguarded conversation, has been caught up and repeated in a way to provoke his anger."

Mrs. Striker now remembered what she had said to Nancy about her grist being deficient in weight; and she mentioned this, without disguise, to her husband.

"That is it, no doubt," said Striker. "Ah me!" he sighed, "that woman does more to make trouble in Cedardale, than anyone else in the village. I've always said this."

"To think I should have been so unguarded!" sighed Mrs. Striker, in a self-upbraiding voice. "O dear! And so I am to blame for what has happened."

Oppressed by this thought, the poor woman buried her face in the bedclothes and sobbed aloud.

"Don't think that I blame you, Hannah," quickly spoke out the blacksmith. "There's no one to blame for my wrong-doing but myself. It will, however, be a warning to you, so far as *Nancy Wimble* is concerned. As for White, let him take care of himself, and not cross my path again. If I'd got my hands on him yesterday, I can't say what would have been the consequences. One thing is certain, he'll grind no more grain for us. There's an honest miller over in Elderglen, and he shall have my business for the future."

Mrs. Striker still remained with her face buried in the bedclothes.

"But this wasn't all," continued her husband. "Not long after White went away, in came *Mary Green*."

"What did *she* want?" asked Mrs. Striker, looking up, and showing tears on her cheeks.

"Why, she came in, as angry as a viper, about her mare Fanny."

"That you lamed in shoeing?"

"Yes. And would you believe it, she wanted me to pay her twenty dollars damages."

"Twenty dollars!" exclaimed his wife.

"It's the truth. She would hear to no reason; and was dreadfully insolent. Of course, I got out of all patience with her, and, at last, unable to stand her sharp tongue any longer, I took her by the arm and led her from the shop. She stood in the road, and screamed out her abuse there for some time, when she went away, threatening all sorts of consequences. This knocked me right down. I remember but little afterward, except that I poured, like a mad fool, at least a pint of liquor down my throat. O dear! I wish I could control myself. But I had a strong provocation, Hannah — very strong. But, God helping me, I will make one more trial."

The light on Mrs. Striker's face was as if the sun had suddenly arisen, and poured his first beams into their chamber-window.

"God will help you, John," she quickly replied. "Oh, try again earnestly. I didn't expect this of Mary Green. I'm sure we both told her that she was welcome to old brown horse whenever she wished to ride. Twenty dollars! What could have given her that idea?"

"*Nancy Wimble* is at the bottom of it, I suppose. She does the mischief-making for the village. I wish to my heart we were well out of it. I've had no good luck since we came here."

The blacksmith then arose, and with more than ordinary calmness of mind, and a resolute purpose to do better, prepared to enter upon another day's work. Mrs. Striker felt again hopeful. Long, long had she looked for a brighter day, and there had often seemed to break in the dark — a precursor of morning; now the black curtain was lifted, she fondly hoped, and day about to dawn.

Thus it was with the blacksmith's family.

As for the *miller*, the rebuff which he had received from Striker fretted him the more, the longer he brooded over it. The outrage was one neither to be forgotten nor forgiven.

"It will cost him dear, or I'm mistaken," said he, as he meditated on schemes of retaliation. "One thing is certain, he gets no more work from me; and I think I've given him about as much as any two others in Cedardale. Elderglen has quite as good a blacksmith, and, I think, a little better. At any rate, he shall set all my picks and facing-hammers after this, and do all the repairs to machinery that I need. Threaten to pitch me, neck and heels, into the road, ha! If he isn't sorry for this before another six months, my name is not Stephen White!"

Although the miller's picks and facing hammers would have lasted him well enough, without calling in the blacksmith's skill, for a week or two longer, so anxious was he to let Striker know that he had lost one good customer, that on the day following the one on which the rebuff was given, he gathered together the dull hammers and broken and worn-out picks, and so arranging them in a meal-bag, that a practiced eye could easily guess what they were, slung them on the saddle-bow of his horse, and started for Elderglen. There were two ways from his mill leading to the Elderglen road; one past Striker's shop, and the other by the mill dam. White purposely chose the former, and was gratified, in passing the smithy, to see Striker standing at the door. The two men glared at each other, but made no signs of recognition.

Halfway to Elderglen, White met a person named Barker, whom he well knew, and also his vocation — that of constable.

"Good day, neighbor Barker — what news?" said he, checking his horse. "Oh, nothing very extraordinary," replied Barker, balancing himself obliquely on his saddle, and drawing one foot from the stirrup, so as to sit at ease while talking.

"We don't give you folks much work in Cedardale," remarked the miller.

"No. At least you haven't done so. But your time is to come yet," and he laughed to himself. "You're not all saints and angels by a mighty deal."

"Never man spoke truer words, friend Barker. We've got some pretty hard subjects, let me tell you; and if some of them aren't in hot water before long, then I'm no prophet. There is John Striker, for instance."

"Striker! He's a pretty hard case, is he?"

"You may well say so. About the hardest case we have."

"I'm just on my way to see him."

"You are!"

"That's my present business. I have a writ for him."

"Good! But what's the matter?"

"Some trouble with Mary Green."

"Ah, ha! He lamed her mare."

"And she has brought suit for damages."

"Good again! He ought to be made to pay well for crippling the poor beast. He was drunk when he did it, of course. But, if men will get drunk, let them pay for the harm they do."

"So say I, friend White. But it seems that Striker was not content with crippling the mare. When Mary called on him yesterday, to ask what he was going to do about it, he not only abused her up and down, right and left, like a blackguard, but actually thrust her out of his shop, bruising her person most shamefully in doing so."

"Well, if that don't beat everything!" exclaimed the miller, who had not yet heard of Mary Green's adventure with the blacksmith. "Threw her out into the road?"

"Yes, and with considerable force, I should conclude," answered the constable.

"He might have injured her for life."

"He may have done so as it is," said the constable. "If I understood aright, she is a good deal hurt."

"Dreadful! Why the man's got the very devil in him!"

"So it seems. But, I guess we'll bring the old 'varmint' out before we're done with him. There will be two suits against him."

"Two!" ejaculated the miller.

"Yes. One for crippling the mare, and one for assault and battery."

"Good!" This was a favorite ejaculation with the miller. "How he will stare when the writs are served! You must look out that he doesn't pitch you into the road. Ha! ha!"

"He'll hardly try that trick!" replied the constable a little gravely, and showing his teeth as he spoke. "But good day, friend White. I have no time to tarry." So, resuming his place in the saddle, Barker spoke to his horse and rode on.

The miller was especially pleased to hear that Striker had got himself into the hands of the law — so well pleased, that he actually drew up his horse several times, before reaching Elderglen; and debated the question, whether to keep on, or to return to Cedardale, and be among the first to spread the news. The calls of business were, however, permitted to hold in abeyance, the miller's inclinations. So he kept on, and in due time arrived at the Elderglen smithy, and made known to Marks, the smith, that in future he was going to patronize him.

"It will cost me more time and trouble, of course," said White. "But you see, friend Marks, Striker has got so drunken, worthless, and ill-natured, that there is no doing anything with him. You have heard, no doubt, how he crippled Mary Green's mare in shoeing her?"

"Oh yes," replied the gratified smith, "I've heard all about that. He must have been very careless."

"Say, rather, very *drunk*," returned the miller.

"As you please about that. In any case, the blunder is unpardonable, and he ought to be made to pay damages."

"Mary Green has *sued* him already," said the miller.

"Ah! has she?"

"Yes, indeed. I met Barker with the writ as I came over this morning."

"I'm sorry for him," remarked the smith. "But it's no more than just."

"I can't say that I'm sorry," rejoined the miller. "I'm sorry for Mary Green. Striker not only crippled her mare, but when she went to see him about it, he abused her shamefully — even going so far as to seize hold of her and throw her into the road. It is thought that she has sustained some bodily injury."

"Is it possible that he has become so outrageous?" said the smith. "Striker used to be a very clever man. But rum spoils everything."

"It has spoiled him, certainly. However, I mustn't be talking here. It takes some time to ride over from Cedardale and back; and no corn can be ground while I am away. When will the picks and facing-hammers be ready?"

"Day after tomorrow," answered Marks.

"Will it be possible for you to send them over?"

"I'm afraid not. Though, if there should be an opportunity, I will certainly embrace it."

"I wish you would. However, I can keep my Ben home from school an afternoon, and let him ride over and get them. It doesn't do for me to be away from the mill, you know; for, when people come with their grain, they expect me to grind it at once. So good day."

"Good day," replied the smith, returning to his forge. The miller left the shop, and mounting his horse, rode off with a brisk trot, not feeling altogether too well satisfied at the prospect of having to go or send a couple of miles every time he had blacksmith's work to do. As for Striker's skill as a mechanic, there was no question on that score; and the miller's tools had ever come from under his hands as perfect as he could ask them. The reputation of Marks did not stand so high by any means; and it rather unpleasantly occurred to the miller, that, possibly, he might lose in more ways than one by the change.

CHAPTER 8

As Mr. White was leaving Elderglen, a horseman drew up to his side, and he instantly recognized the stranger who had called at his mill on the day previous, and to whom he had spoken so freely of the blacksmith.

"The miller of Cedardale, if I'm not mistaken?" said the stranger familiarly.

"That is my vocation," replied Mr. White. "And you are the person who stopped at my mill yesterday."

"The same. But what errand has brought you so far away from home, on a bright day like this, when there will be many grists to grind?"

"Business," replied the miller, while a slight shadow flitted across his face. Then he added, "So much for having a drunken blacksmith in Cedardale."

"What's the matter now?" said the stranger. "Striker is not so intoxicated today, that he cannot work, I hope."

"Not that I know of." The miller tossed his head — "But he's done his last job for me!"

"How is this, friend White? I don't like to hear you say so. If the blacksmith isn't all you could wish him to be, personally, still, as a workman, he should be regarded. Remember, that he has a wife and family, and that, in taking work from him, you take the bread from them."

"Oh, as to his wife, she's no better than he is, if the truth must be told."

"What! Does she *drink* also?"

"Oh no. I don't accuse her of that. But she's got an ill tongue in her head, and says of her neighbors a great deal she ought not to say. And I'm sure this is bad enough."

"Bad enough, no doubt," replied the stranger. "In fact, we are all bad enough. Still, we must have bread to eat. If God were to remove bread from the mouth of every one who sinned against him — we would all, it strikes me, be in rather a bad way."

The miller was silent at this. It was rather a new view of the case to his mind.

"Now, what is all your trouble with the blacksmith?" resumed the stranger. "It occurs to me that there must be wrong on both sides. When I was at his shop yesterday, I could see that he was dreadfully fretted about something."

"I should think he was, from all I saw myself, and from all I have since heard."

"There must have been a *cause* for this," said the stranger. "What was it? I would like to hear, if you can tell me."

"The cause, I presume, was mostly in himself. Drunkenness and ill-nature will account for a good deal of bad conduct in a man. He abused me shamefully, and threatened to pitch me out of his shop, just because I ventured to ask him upon what authority his wife had reported that I double-charged every grist that came to my mill."

"And did she report this?"

"Certainly she did. And I'm not the man to stand anything of that kind, you see. No — no; Stephen White never wronged a neighbor out of a dollar, willingly, and no one shall report such slanderous things of him."

"Who informed you of this?"

"The shoemaker's wife."

"Is she a woman of veracity?"

"Humph! She's the *tattler* and *busybody* of the village — always *meddling* with other people's concerns."

The miller spoke out, warmly, his real appreciation of Nancy Wimble, without thinking of the very natural inference the stranger would draw from his words.

"If that is the case," said the latter, pointedly, "is it not very possible that Nancy Wimble may have *exaggerated*, or entirely misconstrued the blacksmith's wife? And, moreover, wasn't it rather hasty in you to go to Mr. Striker, knowing as you do, so well, his habits and temperament, and complain against his wife? Make the case your own, and ask yourself, if he had come to you, just as you went to him — using precisely the same language, in the same tone of voice — how would you have felt and acted?"

This was putting the case in rather a home way, and the miller felt rebuked. However, he was in no degree inclined to acknowledge his fault, even if convinced of error. So he answered —

"There was nothing to justify his conduct — nothing in the world. But what he did to me was a trifle, compared to the way he treated Mary Green."

"Ah! How did he treat her?"

The story of the lamed mare, and all the consequences growing therefrom, even to the commencement of a suit against the blacksmith, were all related by the miller. The stranger listened with marked interest, and when the narrative was completed, said —

"This is a very bad business, indeed. Who could have incited Mrs. Green to such a course? She will gain little or nothing, and do great harm."

"Striker crippled her mare, and insulted and maltreated her into the bargain," replied the miller. "And he ought to be made to pay for it. I don't blame Mary Green in the least."

"Well, I do then. This going to *law* for mere trifles is always wrong. Who's her lawyer?"

"Sharp, I believe."

"So much the worse," replied the stranger, speaking partly to himself. "All wrong — all wrong," he added musingly, as he reined up his horse, where a road turned off from the one leading to Cedardale.

"My friend," said the stranger, after a pause, "I don't like all this trouble you are getting into very foolishly. This *quarreling among neighbors* seems to me very dreadful. Now, why can't you, instead of helping to *fan these coals of discord* into a consuming flame, act the part of a peacemaker? The matter is very simple. The easiest thing, believe me, imaginable."

"Peacemaker! Goodness!" The miller was taken altogether by surprise. "I'd like to see the man who could harmonize things in Cedardale. He'd be the eighth wonder of the world, to my thinking."

"It requires but one thing, friend White," said the stranger.

"And what is that, please?"

"A sincere desire for the happiness and well-being of your neighbors."

The miller shrugged his shoulders, and said —

"Something hard to find in this world, as far as my experience goes."

"Yet every man should possess it."

"But suppose he does not."

"Let him, then, seek for it earnestly, for, without it, he is no true man," said the stranger. He spoke earnestly, fixing his penetrating eyes upon the miller. The latter felt rebuked and uncomfortable. A word or two, with little significance, he uttered in reply, and then, as he touched the reins of his horse, said —

"But I must bid you good day, sir. Time passes, and my customers will be waiting my return." And bowing, he spoke sharply to the animal he rode, and was quickly beyond the sound of the stranger's voice. The latter gazed after him for some moments, and then moved on his way.

The miller, on entering Cedardale, could not refrain from taking the road which led past the shop of Striker. He was very curious to learn the effect which the serving of the writ had produced. He was not greatly surprised to find the smith absent. He paused and looked narrowly into the shop. Things had a deserted air; the more particularly, as there was no red sign of industry on the forge. The fire had gone out.

"I rather think he's come to his senses by this time," said the miller to himself, as he rode by. There was a sense of *pleasure* in his heart.

On arriving at his mill, "White found three or four people waiting for him, and all of them exceedingly impatient at the delay they had experienced.

"What's the meaning of all this?" said one.

"Where in the world have you been?" asked another.

"You have lost two new customers," remarked a third, "and good ones they would have been, I take it."

"How so! who were they?" inquired the miller to this last remark.

"Why, Glenn, who lives over Beech Hill, and Mr. Weaver, the large farmer. Mr. Weaver brought ten bags of rye to chop, and two bags of wheat to grind; and Glenn had, I would think, as much more."

"Have they gone away?"

"Yes, indeed. And they both said they'd not take the trouble to come over to your mill again. They were here when I came, and said they'd been waiting over an hour. But where in the world have you been, this terrible long while?"

"Over to Elderglen, to the blacksmith's," replied the miller, who felt rather bad at the probable loss of two new customers, whose work would have been of no inconsiderable importance.

"To the blacksmith's!" echoed two or three at once. "What's the matter with Striker?"

"Oh, I'm done with him," replied White. "He's got too drunken, worthless, and ill-natured for anything."

"Aren't you a little mistaken?" was replied by one of those present. "I stopped, as I came past this morning, to get a shoe on my horse, and found him perfectly sober, and in quite a good state of mind."

"Lucky for you that he was," said the miller, "or your horse might now be in the condition of Mary Green's mare. And, by the way, do you know that Mrs. Green has sued him for damages?"

"No," "No," "No," came from several voices at once.

"It's a fact, let me tell you; and I guess he'll come to his senses before he's much older. I met Barker with the writ as I was on my way to Elderglen this morning."

"You don't say so!" "Possible!" "I declare!" and such like exclamations passed round the group of listeners.

"Well, all I've got to say," remarked White, and he spoke with a good deal of feeling, "is, that I hope she'll make him smart. If I was in her place, he'd find himself in trouble, I can assure him."

"All this isn't going to grind my grist," now spoke out one of the miller's customers, who had stood a little aside from the beginning, and taken no part in the conversation. Both in voice and manner, he showed a good deal of impatience. "As to these *quarrels among neighbors*, I don't like them at all. Here are six of us, who have each lost an hour — that makes six hours — just because you and the blacksmith are at loggerheads. If you've got to tramp or ride away over to Elderglen every time you want a bit of smith's work done, I'm thinking you'll find it a business that won't pay. I'm sure I shall not come a third time to your mill, if I find nobody to grind my grist at the second visit."

The miller was rather struck down, as they say, by this speech. So he hurried into the mill, and emptied a bag of wheat into one hopper and a bag of corn into another. Then lifting the gate, he let the water flow down upon the wheel, the buckets of which soon filled, the weight of water setting the wheel in motion. For about five minutes the process of grinding went on, when, suddenly, there was a crash of something among the machinery, and then all became still. The miller, after hastily shutting off the water, went below, in much perturbation, to examine into the nature and extent of the disaster. Greatly to his relief of mind, he found the damage but small, yet of a nature requiring the services of a millwright or some skillful worker in iron.

"I'll go for Striker. He'll soon make all right again," said one of the people present. The miller had it on his tongue's end to object — but prudently forbore. So the man started off for the blacksmith. In about a quarter of an hour he returned, looking serious and disappointed.

"Where's Striker?"

"Wouldn't he come?" asked one and another.

The man shook his head, and seemed reluctant to answer in

words.

"He won't work for me, I suppose," suggested White. "That's about the truth of it."

"No," said the other; "the truth of it is, he's in no condition to work for anybody."

"He was sober enough when he shod my horse this morning," remarked one.

"And would have kept sober, no doubt, but for the serving of that writ," said the man who had, a little while before, expressed his disapprobation of neighbors' quarrels. "I wouldn't have Mary Green's responsibility in this matter for a dozen horses. I'm out of all patience with her. I gave her credit for being a better woman. But she's among bad advisers, I suppose. Ah, well! It's sad to think on. However, finding fault won't mend things; and as there is no more grinding to be done here today, I must be off in the direction of Elderglen, for there is no meal in the barrel, and my wife will hardly look pleasant if I return as I left."

Saying this, the man lifted his bag of grain, and throwing it over his horse, mounted, and rode away. His example was soon followed by all the rest, and the miller was left alone with his silent mill and his no very pleasant reflections. The way before him was apparent enough, but not very pleasant to walk in. He must return to Elderglen, and get the blacksmith there to come or send over and see his broken machinery. Then there would be delay in taking the portions needing repairs a distance of two miles, and afterwards bringing them back to the mill.

As no time was to be lost in musing over his troubles, Mr. White started forthwith on his second journey to Elderglen. But he found the smith there too busy to attend to him on that day. A promise to call over on the next morning was all he could obtain. As it turned out, two entire days were lost by the miller, before he was able to set his great wheel to moving again; when, if the aid of Striker could have been secured at once, scarcely two hours would have been consumed in the work of repairs.

"I wonder where Ben White is, this afternoon?" said Martin, the schoolmaster, on the day after the mill went into operation again. He spoke to Dick Wimble, who had been kept in for bad conduct, after the other scholars were dismissed, and was now alone with his teacher.

"I guess he's played truant," answered Dick.

"Why do you think so?" asked the schoolmaster, pricking up his ears, and showing sufficient interest to prompt the shoemaker's son to make as good a story as possible.

"I saw him on my way to school, and he said he wasn't going to come."

"Why not?"

"He said he was going to Elderglen, and wanted me to go along."

"To Elderglen?"

"Yes, sir."

"And you think he meant to play truant?" said the schoolmaster.

"I'm most sure he did," replied Dick.

Taking rather too much for granted, the schoolmaster, on the next morning, as soon as Ben White appeared, called him up, and in a tone of voice which plainly indicated a foregone conclusion, said —

"And so you went over to Elderglen, yesterday afternoon?"

"Yes, sir," replied Ben, the blood mounting to his face; for the tone and manner of the schoolmaster startled him with some undefined apprehension.

"Very well, sir!" The master's voice was stern, and his eyes full of fire and accusation. "And what were you doing over there?"

By this time Ben was so borne down by a sudden fear and confusion, occasioned by this unexpected arraignment, that guilt, or what Martin interpreted as guilt, was written all over his countenance.

"Father sent me there," he replied in a faltering voice, his eyes falling under those of the schoolmaster.

"Your father sent you, ha?"

"Yes, sir."

"What for?"

"I went to the blacksmith's for him."

"To the blacksmith's, indeed!" rejoined the schoolmaster, incredulously. "That's a likely story, when there's a blacksmith in Cedardale. And what was your business at the blacksmith's? Now, take care how you answer, boy, for, remember, you can't deceive me; and if I'm satisfied that you're lying, I'll take the very skin off you."

"I went after father's picks and facing-hammers," said the frightened boy, in a troubled manner, and looking still more confused — or guilty, as the schoolmaster thought.

"That'll do," rejoined Martin. "That'll do! Picks and facing-hammers, indeed! You should have tried a better story. To my own knowledge, Mr. Striker always does that work for your father. Doesn't he, Bill?"

"Yes, sir," faintly and reluctantly replied the blacksmith's son.

"There, you see! you're convicted at once," said the now morally blind schoolmaster. "Picks and facing-hammers, indeed! You were playing truant — that's what you were doing!"

And as he spoke, he laid his hand with a strong grip on the lad's arm, at the same time reaching over to his desk for a stout hickory rod.

"Oh, indeed, sir, I didn't play truant! It's all just as I said," pleaded the miller's son. "Father did send me over to Elderglen; indeed he did, Mr. Martin! Oh! don't whip me, sir. Send down to father, and he'll tell you all about it."

But, in the schoolmaster's mind, the question was settled. He was no longer *judge*, but *executioner*. Before the last words trembled from the lips of young White, the hand of Martin had fallen, and the sharp strokes of his rod were thrilling on the ears of his scholars, sending the quick blood to the faces of some, and blanching the cheeks of others.

"Now, sir, go to your seat! Playing truant may be all very fine, but there's something not so pleasant to come afterward," said the schoolmaster, after having flogged the poor boy until his arm was tired. As he spoke, he thrust him toward the row of benches and desks in front of him, with so strong an arm, that Ben came near falling upon his face. Quickly recovering himself, however, he darted from the school-room, and sped away for home with almost lightning feet.

This act on the part of young White rather disturbed the schoolmaster, as soon as his thoughts ran a little clear. If it should really be true that the miller had sent his son over to Elderglen, there would be trouble. Not very long was Martin in doubt. Barely sufficient time had elapsed for Ben — who had suffered innocently — to reach the mill, where he exhibited his bruises and swollen back, and for the miller to walk to the school-house, before Martin's growing apprehensions were realized.

Of the scene that ensued we will not venture a description. But for the appearance of the stranger before mentioned, who happened to be riding past the schoolhouse most opportunely, and who, hearing angry voices within, dismounted and entered, the terribly excited miller would have punished the schoolmaster with blows.

CHAPTER 9

Unhappy drunkard's wife! How suddenly overclouded was your sky again! How gloomily fell the shadows upon your threshold, where, a little while before, the sunlight played with so bright a promise.

"Be a man, John — be strong," said Mrs. Striker to her husband, as he was about leaving for his day's work on the morning after his trouble with the miller and Mary Green. And the long-suffering wife laid her hand upon his arm, and looked earnestly, yet with hopeful tenderness, in his face.

"I will, Hannah! I will," replied the blacksmith. He spoke with much feeling. "God helping me, I will become a new man."

And with such resolute words, he turned from his wife and walked away, with a light footstep, for his shop.

"Amen! God help you!" This was the heartfelt ejaculation of Mrs. Striker, as she parted from her husband; and, with a warmer glow in her bosom than she had felt for many a day, resumed her household duties. There had been unusual quiet through the house during this morning. Too often it happened that differences and disputes among the children, generally excited by William, the eldest son, kept all in a state of discord until he was fairly off for school.

"What can have come over the boy?" said Mrs. Striker to herself, as she observed him give place to one of the younger children at table, during the morning meal, and yield up a favorite piece to another who expressed a wish to have it. And the question was repeated to herself, wonderingly, again, after her husband left for his work, on seeing him make an effort, and a successful one, too, to reconcile a little brother and sister who had got into a dispute. A short time afterward she said to him —

"Isn't it school-time, William?"

Now, it was the invariable custom of this boy, who had seemed given over to a *perverse* and *disobedient* spirit, to oppose his mother's wishes, and seek to disobey her commands in everything. To her expressed desire that he would start for school in the morning, he never failed to reply, that it wasn't time; or, that he didn't want to go to school; and it required, on her part, repeated injunctions, and often threats of punishment, before he could be induced to start. A new surprise and gratification now awaited the mother.

"Yes, mother," promptly answered the boy, leaving his play — he was amusing himself with the younger children — and commencing at once to gather up his books. In a little while he started off, whistling merrily.

"I wonder what has come over the child," murmured Mrs. Striker, as she stood looking after him, affected with a new surprise at seeing him walk briskly along, instead of loitering to throw stones and amuse himself in other ways, as was his almost invariable custom. The boy had said nothing of the interview with the *stranger* on the previous day, and she had, therefore, no clue to *unravel the mystery* of this sudden change.

The hours of the morning glided pleasantly away, and so lightly beat the pulses of Mrs. Striker, that, before noontime came, she was actually singing at her work. As the line of shadow on the window-sill marked the hour of twelve, the last dish was placed on the dinner-table, and a better meal for her husband than usual stood hot by the fire, ready to be served at the moment of his entrance.

"See if your father is coming," said she to one of the children. "It's past twelve."

The child ran to the gate and looked down the road.

"Do you see him?" called the mother.

"No, mother," replied the child. "But *Bill* is coming."

"Coming all alone?" There was a shade of disappointment and anxiety in the voice of Mrs. Striker.

"Yes, mother," was answered.

Now, as, in returning from school, the boy had to pass the blacksmith-shop, and very often came home with his father — though more commonly a little later — the fact of his coming alone caused an uneasy feeling to pervade the bosom of Mrs. Striker. The throbbing of her heart became more and more distinct every moment, as she awaited the arrival of William.

"Where is your father?" she inquired in a tone of anxiety that she strove, though in vain, to conceal.

"I don't know," replied the boy. "I thought he had come home."

"Were you at the shop?"

"Yes, mother."

"Wasn't anyone there?"

"No, mother; and it didn't look as if there had been anybody there for a good while. The fire was all out on the forge."

Mrs. Striker dropped suddenly into a chair. Her strength left her in a moment. The boy looked at her with a sober face for a little while, and then said —

"Shall I go over to Joe Parker's tavern, and see if he is there?"

Mrs. Striker did not reply. How could she say "Yes."

"Say, mother, shall I go? I expect he's there. Maybe he doesn't know it's so late."

The lad lingered for a short time, but, as his mother, who sat almost as immovable as stone, with her eyes fixed on vacancy, did not answer, he started off, determined to find his father, if possible, and bring him home.

Nancy Wimble, who had learned, nearly two hours before, that a writ had been served on the blacksmith at the instance of Mary Green, and who had, in that time, spread the news over the whole village, could not resist, as she passed near Striker's, just to step in a moment, and see how things looked, even if a later dinner for her hungry husband was the consequence. As William passed through the gate, to go after his father, she entered, and, coming into the house, found Mrs. Striker in the position and state we have described.

"How do you do, Mrs. Striker?" said she.

Mrs. Striker lifted her head, and merely remarked in a cold, absent manner —

"Well, Nancy."

The shoemaker's wife stood for a few moments, gazing upon the pale, suffering face of Mrs. Striker, and, as she did so, she felt rebuked for the part she had taken in prompting Mrs. Green to commence a suit against the blacksmith.

"I wouldn't take on so about it, Hannah," said she. "It's my opinion that Mary Green can't recover a cent."

At these words there was an instant change in Mrs. Striker. She startled, while a flash of inquiry lighted her countenance.

"Mary Green! What of her? What has she done?" she asked eagerly.

"Why, I thought you knew all about it. Hasn't your husband told you?"

"Told me what? Oh, Nancy! Speak out plainly at once."

"Why, that Mary Green has commenced a suit against him for assault and battery, as well as for crippling her mare. Constable Barker came over from Elderglen this morning, and served the writ."

"Constable — writ — assault and battery!" echoed Mrs. Striker, in a bewildered manner, while she clasped her hands across her forehead. "Oh dear! What has happened, Nancy? What does it all mean? Where is my poor husband? They haven't carried him off, have they?"

"Oh no, I reckon not," replied Nancy. "He doesn't have to appear at the squire's until next week; so I heard from Mr. Barker, who called to see Samuel after he had served the writ."

This quieted, in a measure, the vague alarm which Nancy's words had created; though it took nothing from the heavy weight that rested on her feelings.

"I thought I'd run in a moment, as I was going by, and see how you were," resumed Nancy, "and just give my opinion of Mary Green. Isn't it awful for a neighbor to do so; particularly as you had given her the use of your horse whenever she wanted to ride? I never had much opinion of her, anyhow. But no good will come to her, take my word for it!"

"Oh dear! There's nothing but trouble!" sighed Mrs. Striker. She spoke rather to herself than for the ears of an auditor. "And to think that it should have happened just now!"

"I wouldn't take on so about it," said Nancy. "I don't believe she can do anything. Her old mare isn't worth twenty dollars, hide and hair and all. So I've heard a dozen people say this morning — and so I say. She's forgotten about her cow breaking into your garden and eating up your whole bed of young cabbages, and doing, Heaven above knows, how much damages. If I was Mr. Striker, I'd bring a suit against her — that I would. Two can play at this game, you know, as well as one."

But if the blacksmith's wife heard all this, she made no answer; and, as it was already past Nancy's dinner-time, the latter, after a few more *comforting words*, took her departure. Scarcely had she gone before Mrs. Striker left the house, and, going to the garden-gate, looked anxiously along the road in the direction of Joe Parker's tavern — a place to which her husband too frequently resorted. She was not long in suspense, for soon a boy and a man were seen in the distance — the boy leading the man, and evidently making use of considerable effort to guide his steps safely and steadily. Her practiced eyes at once recognized her husband and son.

Shortly they drew near, and, at last, were at the garden-gate, where still stood the wife and mother. Striker, intoxicated as he was, remembered the assurances of a better life which he had given in the morning, and as he staggered through the gate, muttered with eyes averted —

"It's no sort of use for me to try, Hannah. They won't let me do right, if I would."

And so he passed on into the house. Slowly and with unsteady steps, Mrs. Striker followed. The last prop upon which she had leaned, appeared taken from under her. A newly-awakened hope had gone out in utter darkness; and to sudden sickness of mind, came sickness of body. Nature was tried too far. She uttered no word; shed no tear; there came not from her lips either sigh or moan; but, as the boy guided his half-stupefied parent into a chamber, she ascended to a little spare room above, and when, shortly after, he went to seek her, she was lying upon the bed, her face cold and rigid, and white as death!

Stricken with alarm at so terrible a sight for his young eyes, the boy, after recovering from his first bewilderment of mind, ran off for their nearest neighbor, whom he startled by the weeping announcement that his mother was dead. Hurriedly obeying this summons, the neighbor repaired to the dwelling of the blacksmith. She found poor Mrs. Striker still insensible; but soon, by the use of cold water and other appliances, succeeded in recalling her again to conscious life. But the renewed pulsations of her heart sent fever, instead of health, through her veins; while her physical system was so entirely prostrate that, when she made an effort to rise, her head swam dizzily, and she sank back, feeling utterly powerless, upon her pillow. That would have been a hard heart, which was not touched by the moan of anguish that breathed from her colorless lips.

CHAPTER 10

The reader will be in no way surprised to hear that, in consequence of the school-master's hasty condemnation and unjust punishment of the miller's son, he lost a scholar — or rather, we should say three scholars; for Mr. White had three children in Martin's school, all of whom were removed forthwith.

On the morning after the exciting scene, which, but for the timely appearance of the stranger, would have been even more exciting, and, in all probability, led to a lawsuit between the miller and the school-master, Bill Striker, the blacksmith's son, happened to be one of the first scholars who appeared at the school-house.

"Wasn't it Dick Wimble who told me, yesterday, that Ben White had been playing truant?" said Martin to the lad.

"Yes, sir," replied young Striker.

"He must have known better," said the schoolmaster, speaking partly to himself.

"And he did know better," unhesitatingly replied Striker.

"What reason, have you for saying this?" was very naturally asked.

"I heard Dick say, after school, that *he'd* got Ben White one good thrashing. That he knew well enough that his father had sent him to Elderglen, for he was riding his horse, and had some picks in a bag. But that he owed him a grudge, and you too — and that now he was satisfied."

This was all true; and so the school-master received it. The lesson of the day before, on the subject of hasty judgment and a too prompt action therefrom, was now forgotten in the anger excited against Wimble. The moment the boy appeared, he was arraigned. Two or three scholars confirming, in part, the allegation of Striker, swift and severe punishment came. The jacket of the boy had been taken off, and the rod of Martin, having in it two or three rough protuberances, broke the skin in several places on his back, while the bruises were many in number. The exhibition of these bruises and lacerations at home, accompanied by *Dick's own version* of his offence, produced another explosion, and another diminution of scholars in the village-school. Three of the shoemaker's children were removed.

Thus the trouble increased. In Nancy Wimble, the school-master found an active enemy. The mere removal of her own children was not regarded as by any means a sufficient satisfaction for the wrong alleged to have been done to her boy. She was bent on driving the schoolmaster out of Cedardale, and filling his place with, as she was pleased to say, "another and a better man." And before a week had elapsed, she was in a fair way to accomplish her purpose, having in that brief time influenced three families to withdraw their children from his school.

Martin was now becoming seriously alarmed, and set himself to work to counteract the movements of Nancy Wimble. In this, his wife, who was a pretty free and not over-scrupulous talker, joined him in good earnest. Their "bread and butter was in danger," and this was reason sufficient to induce an active opposition on their part; and they soon had the satisfaction of knowing, that if the school-room showed a poorer attendance of scholars, the ringing of Wimble's hammer on his lapstone was far less incessant than before, and that a certain maker and mender of shoes in Elderglen had received a material increase of custom. Their boast of this, as an effect produced by themselves, coming to the ears of the Wimbles, aroused them to new activity.

On the other hand, the aid of Sharp, the lawyer, was invoked by the Martins. From him they gained the information, that Wimble and his wife could be prosecuted for *libel and defamation of character*, which had resulted in material detriment to themselves. So he was instructed forthwith to have suits commenced against these offending parties. This was all in Sharp's line of business; and, accordingly, the suits were brought. So, here was more trouble for Cedardale and its inhabitants.

Meantime poor Striker had fallen, it was feared, not to rise again. His only sober time was in the morning; while night after night found him drunk to utter insensibility. He was worse, in fact, than he had ever been before. The only time that any work could be got out of him, was early in the forepart of the day; and it usually happened that nearly all the money he received was spent for liquor before night. Mrs. Striker remained sick, and her children sadly neglected. The miller and his wife, who both continued to feel very much incensed toward Mr. and Mrs. Striker, had influence enough to keep up an active prejudice among a large number of the villagers, and thus obstruct the humane consideration and attention which the sick and heart-broken woman would have received.

The baleful effects of so sad a state of antagonism as was exhibited at Cedardale, soon manifested itself in a way to affect, more or less intimately, every one of its inhabitants. The miller refused to employ the blacksmith, the shoemaker, and the schoolmaster, and these, in turn, not only refused to employ him, but each other. More than one-half of the people were either suffering inconvenience or wasting their time in running over to Elderglen to get work done or make purchases. In consequence, the mill-wheel stood dry and motionless in the sun, for more than half the time, while the bright water, unused, went foaming over the dam; the fire died on the blacksmith's forge; the shoemaker sat smoking for hours before his door, or wandered off to seek companionship at the tavern; while the schoolmaster contemplated, with no pleasant feelings, his more than half-emptied desks and benches. Even the storekeeper, who had kept a closer tongue than usual, while he listened to all, offended in consequence of not taking sides, and lost custom both in this way and because people who went to Elderglen on other business took occasion to purchase dry goods and groceries while there, under the impression that they could buy to more advantage. This latter impression was encouraged by the Elderglen storekeeper, who sold certain articles below cost, in order to create a talk in Cedardale, and get up a reputation for cheapness. So the storekeeper in Cedardale suffered equally with the rest, and perhaps a little beyond them.

Thus matters remained for a long enough time to produce serious distress in the village; yet there was no one to come forward as a *true peacemaker*, and seek, from an unselfish regard for the good of the whole, to bring order and harmonious action out of these conflicting elements; and those who were in the bitterness of antagonism cherished, rather than strove to give up, that baleful hatred of their neighbor, under the dominion of which they had so entirely come.

One day, some weeks after this unhappy state of affairs had reached a most alarming climax, and one and another began to ask, in low, trembling voices, where it was all to end; Nancy Wimble, who had been unable to learn how the case of Mary Green and the blacksmith stood, paid a visit to the former, in order to have her curiosity fully satisfied. She found that Mrs. Green, who had already paid the lawyer, for fees, serving writ, etc., over twelve dollars, was getting rather sick of the business. But she probed the festering sore, and succeeded in exciting renewed feelings of bitterness towards the blacksmith. After settling this, the main purpose of her errand, she said —

"Didn't I see the windows of the old Markland house open, as I came along?"

This was a fine old mansion, not far from Mrs. Green's, which had been unoccupied for years; the owner having died, and the heirs, who lived at a distance, becoming involved in a lawsuit respecting the settlement of the estate. This suit had recently been brought to a close, and the property, which included a fine farm, thrown into the market.

"I shouldn't wonder if you did," replied Mary Green. "The property has been sold."

"You don't tell me!" responded Nancy. "Then that lawsuit is ended?"

"So I presume."

""Who has bought the property?"

"A gentleman named Trueman, I hear."

"Trueman? Trueman? Who is he, I wonder?"

"He's of the family of Truemans who live in Elderglen."

"Oh! Ah! Indeed! Is he? Well, they are not much to brag of. I wonder if he's going to occupy it himself?"

"So I have been told."

"Humph!" Nancy tossed her head and curled her lips. "They are a stuck-up set, those Truemans, the whole of them."

Mary Green not responding to this, Nancy ran on with a good deal more, in *disparagement* of the Truemans, and ended by saying, that if they did not carry themselves pretty straight in Cedardale, they would soon find themselves in hot water.

In returning home, the shoemaker's wife could not resist the strong inclination she felt to call at the old Markland house, especially as many signs of inhabitants, not before noticed, were now apparent to her closer observation. As she approached the large entrance to the mansion, along the graveled walk, she was met by a middle-aged, thoughtful-looking gentleman, with a countenance strangely familiar, who said, "Good day, madam," in a tone so respectful and kind, that she experienced an instant bias in his favor. He then asked her to walk into the house, which invitation she accepted. The ample parlor into which she was taken, had the newly-introduced furniture all arranged; and there were present two ladies — one in the meridian, and the other in the sweet May-morning of life. To these Nancy was presented, and they received her with an easy dignity and a kindness of manner which quite overcame her. Self-possessed and assured as she was under most circumstances, she felt a good deal confused now, and it was some moments after she was seated before she could collect her thoughts to say —

"I hope you will excuse me for calling; but seeing the old house, which has so long been empty, once more inhabited, I thought I would just drop in, and ask if I could be of any service."

"We are certainly very much obliged to you," replied the elder of the two ladies, in a mild, penetrating voice; yet gazing so fixedly into the face of Nancy, that the eyes of the latter sank under the intelligent scrutiny. Then she added —

"We are strangers here, and shall, of course, feel indebted for any kindnesses which may be extended toward us."

Nancy, in spite of her struggles to regain her self-possession, felt embarrassed. There was something in the presence of the ladies that caused a feeling of uneasiness almost suffocating. Before she replied to the last remark, the speaker added —

"You have one of the most beautiful villages I have ever seen; and I trust we shall find the hearts of its inhabitants in accord with the harmonies of nature."

To this, Nancy replied —

"Cedardale, ma'am, is a lovely spot, certainly. As for the *people*, however, they are no better than you will find in other places. It takes all sorts, you know, to make a world."

"You belong to the village, of course?" said the gentleman, who had remained silent from the time of his entrance, yet reading her face carefully.

"Oh yes, sir," answered Nancy, turning her eyes toward the speaker, and now, for the first time, recognizing the stranger, to whom, not many weeks before, she had given so discouraging an account of the denizens of Cedardale.

"Mrs. Wimble, the shoemaker's wife, I believe?" he added.

"Yes, sir." The color rose over the neck and face of Nancy, in spite of her efforts to prevent it.

"I hope," said the gentleman, "that we shall find things in rather a better condition than they were a few weeks ago, when I called, as you may remember, at your house. Have the miller and blacksmith settled their difficulty?"

"Oh no!" quickly answered Nancy. "And what's more, *never* will."

"Never is a long time," was gravely answered to this.

"It isn't long enough for them to come together, by a great deal. And not much matter, at best. No great deal will be lost; for Striker is going to the dogs as fast as he can go."

"What's the matter with him?"

"He's drunk all the time."

"What does his poor family do?" asked one of the ladies, in a voice of real sympathy.

"Heaven knows! I am not on good terms with Mrs. Striker; and haven't been to her house for these two or three weeks. She's been sick; and I don't know that she's much better now."

"Poor woman!" said the lady with manifest concern. "If ifs so bad with her husband, as you say, I don't wonder that she is sick. Where does she live?"

"In the little red house, with a garden in front, just where the road turns off to go to the mill," replied Nancy.

"We must send down and see if she doesn't need something," remarked the elder of the two ladies, speaking aside to her daughter, for that was the relation between them.

Nancy heard this, and felt it as a rebuke. In self-justification she said —

"I'm sure I'd do anything I could for Mrs. Striker; but the last time I called there, she snapped me up in a way that was not at all agreeable. I have feelings as well as other people. And, besides, I don't care about offering a *bone* to a dog that may bite my fingers off while taking it. If you'll heed the advice of one who knows," added Nancy Wimble, "you'll not be too familiar with Hannah Striker. She's as proud as Lucifer; and, if you make an offer of kindness, will, most likely, tell you she is no pauper. I know her like a book."

The ladies merely glanced at each other, without making any reply. Nancy did not see the peculiar look that was exchanged. Fairly on her *hobby*, and now stimulated by a question from the gentleman, she entered pretty freely upon the personal history and characteristics of the villagers, not one of whom she spared. This *work of slander and depreciation* finished, Nancy, who, from the remarks that followed, was pretty well assured that her auditors did not think too highly of her, as a *defamer*, took her departure.

"I'm most sorry I said so much," she remarked to herself, as, with a feeling of wounded self-esteem, she left the house and took her way homeward. "But they'll soon find out for themselves. Let them go or send to Hannah Striker, and, my word for it, they'll get enough of her."

The oftener Nancy Wimble turned over in her thoughts the kind of reception she had met with from the Truemans, the less did she feel satisfied. It was very plain that they had not formed quite so good an opinion of her as she entertained of herself; and the longer this unpleasant consciousness remained, the stronger and stronger became her feelings of dislike toward them. With Nancy, to *feel*, was to *talk*. But in the present state of misunderstanding and separation in Cedardale, to whom could she talk? The number was small. Still, by communicating to these *her impression of the new-comers*, that impression would soon pass from lip to lip, and thus make the circuit of the village in a short time.

So, she forthwith began her work. Anticipating an early visit from Mrs. Trueman, or her daughter, to the blacksmith's wife, and very naturally apprehending a different reception from the one she had prophesied — a result that would still further lessen her in their good opinion — she determined to let go for nothing, a most positive assertion that she would "never darken Mrs. Striker's door again' and make her first visit of detraction to her. This was accordingly done.

CHAPTER 11

The case of Mary Green against the blacksmith had come to trial before a justice of the peace as often as twice; but, each time, the lawyers employed by the two parties managed, on one pretense or other, to get it postponed. By this means, both were enabled to increase their fees. On each occasion Striker had returned so stupid from drink, that he scarcely knew his own house when he arrived at home, and for several following days did not do a stroke of work. The third trial of the case was to take place at ten o'clock on the day following that on which Nancy Wimble called at the old Markland house, as mentioned in the preceding chapter; and the blacksmith was nursing his bitter feelings against Mrs. Green, and vowing, in his heart, to spend every dollar he could "make and scrape together in the world — would be cast in the approaching trial." He knew more of law and legal proceeding, than he had ever known in his life before, and talked of little else.

As for Mrs. Striker, she was recovering but slowly from the utter prostration of mind and body that took place when the warm light of hope for the future which had fallen around her with so cheering a presence, went suddenly out in darkness. For nearly a week she kept her bed. When, at last, she was able to rise, and go about the house for a short time each day, it was with such feeble and tottering steps, and such a sense of weakness, that she could not keep back the tears which a thought of her helplessness, amid so many duties, brought ever to her eyes.

Day by day passed, and the unhappy woman seemed scarcely to gain anything in physical strength, and nothing occurred to bring a ray of comfort to her mind. She was, besides, apparently deserted by all her friends. No one came to aid or comfort her in her weakness and sorrow — no one sent even with a message of kind words, as had been the aforetime custom in Cedardale, when a neighbor was sick or in feeble health, some little delicacy to tempt the capricious appetite. Alone she stood, while the burden she strove to carry was crushing her hopelessly to the earth.

And so the weary, tearful, despairing time wore on for Mrs. Striker; the *clouds*, instead of showing a rift, were it ever so small, through which the sky above could be seen — becoming thicker and darker. She had arisen from her bed, one day, scarcely refreshed, after having, in utter exhaustion, thrown herself down an hour before, about the middle of the afternoon, and had seated herself by a table on which was a large pile of clothes to clean and fold, preparatory to their being ironed. This was on the same day that Nancy Wimble paid her visit to Mary Green and to the Truemans. The arms of the poor woman, as she rested them on the table, felt as if they were of lead — so heavy and shorn of vitality did they seem; and it was with an effort that she could support herself in her chair.

"Oh dear! oh dear!" she sighed, as her head sank down to the level of the table, and rested on her hands, "What shall I do? What is to become of us?"

The latch of the garden-gate clicked at this moment. Mrs. Striker raised her head, and glanced from the window. Two strange ladies were entering from the road.

"Who can they be?" she said wonderingly; and as they approached along the path which led to the house, she made a hurried effort to restore to partial order, the disarranged furniture of the room.

In a moment or two came a low knock at the door, which she opened.

"Mrs. Striker?" said the elder of the visitors, in a mild voice, and with a smile on her face that made the blacksmith's wife feel instantly that a friend stood before her.

"Will you walk in?" she replied, in a tone and with a manner that at once dispelled from the minds of her visitors, who were none other than Mrs. Trueman and her daughter, all *doubts* as to their reception — doubts which the remarks of Nancy Wimble had very naturally created.

The two ladies entered, and so soon as seated, the elder of them said —

"We have just moved into the village, my name is Mrs. Trueman, and this is my daughter; we have taken the house and farm that used to be owned by the Marklands. Hearing a little while ago that you were sick, we have called over to see if there is anything that we can do for you. So, you will excuse our seeming intrusion."

And the lady smiled with so pleasant a smile, and there was such a look of true humanity on her face, that Mrs. Striker's heart was drawn to her instantly.

"You are very kind," she murmured, while a slight flush came into her pale cheeks. "Very kind — and I thank you."

This was gently said, and in a grateful voice.

"Have you been sick long?" inquired the younger of the two visitors — Mary Trueman. She had not spoken before. Instantly the feelings of Mrs. Striker went out toward her, as they had already gone out toward her mother. She felt that she was in the presence of true friends; that she was not altogether deserted in her sorrow and despair. The thought melted her feelings, as was seen in her slightly quivering lips, and unsteady voice, when she answered—
"A few weeks."
She did not venture to say more; but reserved her words until self-possession was regained.
"What has ailed you?" now inquired Mrs. Trueman.
Although Mrs. Striker's eyes remained fixed on those of her questioner, she did not reply. Once or twice there was a motion of the lips, as if she were about to answer; but the silence continued until a slight sense of embarrassment began to creep over the feelings of both Mrs. Trueman and her daughter. The former was about making some remark on a new subject, when she observed tears pressing out from the eyes of Mrs. Striker, who was, evidently, struggling hard to conceal emotions that were too powerful for restraint, and began to fall, in quickly succeeding drops, over her cheeks.
"We are friends; and I am sure you will find us, in the end, *real* friends," said Mrs. Trueman, drawing her chair close to that of Mrs. Striker, and laying her hand upon hers. "We are here to offer service and good-will."
Scarcely were these words spoken, before the heart of Mrs. Striker gave way. A few quivering sobs ran through her slender frame, and then, with a low moan, or rather cry, she bent forward and leaned her weeping face upon her visitor.
A deep silence succeeded to this. Then such gentle and encouraging words as Mrs. Trueman could utter, were spoken. Calmness and self-possession came in their own good time. Before the two ladies went out from the humble dwelling of the blacksmith, they knew the history of his life, and understood clearly his present relations and the unhappy condition of his family; and what was more, and better, they were resolved, if it were possible, to change the one and improve the other.
Scarcely had they departed, before Nancy Wimble came in. But she was too late to do *harm*. Though she talked against and sneered at the Truemans as "proud," "upstarts," and "meddlesome," she did not succeed in planting a single germ of ill-will, suspicion, car dislike, in the mind of her neighbor, whose heart had unfailingly

recognized the genuine kindness and real purpose to do good in the characters of her recent visitors.

"I only wish," was her simple, rather distantly spoken reply to Nancy's censures, "that we had a few more in Cedardale like them. We should all be much better and happier than we now are."

Nancy curled her lip, and tossed her head at this, and prophesied that there would be a "change of tune" on the part of Mrs. Striker before many weeks passed over. After abusing the schoolmaster and his wife in the bitterest manner, and imparting the information, in a tone evincing inward pleasure, that the school was nearly broken up, and the family getting into very straitened circumstances, she went away, and left Mrs. Striker in a more cheerful state than she had been for many weeks.

"What is done must be done quickly," said Mrs. Trueman to her daughter, as they walked homeward from their visit to Mrs. Striker. "I must try and see Mrs. Green today, and use my best efforts to dissuade her from a further prosecution of this suit."

"She may think it a most unjustifiable *interference* on your part," returned the daughter. "We are but strangers in the village, you know; and must be a little on our guard. People are naturally sensitive about new-comers."

"True enough, Mary. I shall have to move with circumspection. But, as things are so near a crisis, the worst can only come from inaction. Something must be risked when matters assume a position like the present."

Even while the mother and daughter were thus conversing, Mary Green, who had received a note from Sharp, the lawyer, desiring to see her at his office to consult about the trial which was to take place on the next day, was preparing to visit Elderglen. Fanny was not, of course, in a state to be ridden; and so Mrs. Green had to depend, for a horse, on one of her neighbors. The blacksmith's old brown horse was out of the question; and she was not on her usual good terms with the miller. Application was, therefore, first made in another quarter; but the owner of the animal she wished to borrow having had a misunderstanding with the shoemaker, was just preparing to ride over to Elderglen to get shoes for himself and one of his boys; and his wife was to accompany him in order to buy some groceries and dry goods, which she imagined could be purchased on better terms than in Cedardale — forgetful of the fact that even if a few pennies were saved, dollars were thrown away in loss of time. So Mary Green was disappointed here; and a like disappointment attended every other application. There was not a single owner of a horse for which she asked, who was not preparing to ride over to *Elderglen* on some business or other.

In this dilemma, it occurred to Mrs. Green that, probably, her new neighbors, the Truemans, might be willing to let her have a horse for a few hours. She did not wish to intrude on them for a favor, so early after their arrival in Cedardale; but then her visit to Elderglen could not be delayed, even if she had to go the whole distance there and back on foot. After a good deal of thought on the subject, she finally made up her mind to call on the Truemans and ask them, as a great favor, to lend her one of their horses for a few hours. So she put on her things, and started for the old Markland house, which was not very far distant.

CHAPTER 12

Mrs. Trueman and her daughter had been home a short time, and were still in conference about the unhappy condition of affairs in the village, when a *visitor* was announced. A middle-aged woman, with a mild, not over-expressive face, was shown in, and the ladies were rather taken by surprise when she mentioned her name as *Mrs. Green*. In the blacksmith's prosecutor, they had pictured to themselves quite a different personage.

"A golden opportunity," said Mrs. Trueman to herself, with that genuine emotion of pleasure which is felt by a true lover of the neighbor, at the prospect of doing good. Then advancing toward her visitor, she received her with a frankness and courtesy that instantly won her heart. Before Mrs. Green made known her errand, Mrs. Trueman had taken occasion to allude to her recent visit to the blacksmith's wife. She saw that a *shadow* instantly fell over the mild face of Mary Green; but as the subject was now opened, she determined to pursue it, trusting for a favorable issue.

"Poor woman," she remarked in a tone of genuine feeling, "I don't know when my sympathies for anyone have been so much excited. Broken down in mind and body; a family of children claiming her care, thought, and labor; neglected by old friends and neighbors, afflicted with a drunken husband — can you, Mrs. Green, imagine a condition more painful? Ah! if you had seen her white face today, as I saw it; her weakened frame, bending under its own weight, as she moved with uneven steps about the room; if you had heard, in sad, broken tones, as I did, the story of her weakness and hopelessness — your heart must have been wet with tears. Mine was."

Mrs. Green had *feelings*, and they did not lie very far below the surface; she had a *conscience*, too, not inaccessible to words of reproof. Already she was touched with pity for poor Mrs. Striker, and rebuked for what she had done toward adding to a burden already too heavy to be borne without weariness and pain.

"She has been sick," was her remark. She only spoke because there seemed to be a necessity for saying something.

"Quite sick, and ought to be in bed now," replied Mrs. Trueman. "But, is it not very strange, Mrs. Green, that her neighbors have not called in during her sickness to see her and help her? What can it mean? Why, even if she were the vilest of the vile, *common humanity* would dictate a different course from this!"

"Her husband has made himself very offensive to everybody in the village," said Mrs. Green, a flush coming into her face.

"Men who drink are very apt, while in liquor, to give offence to their neighbors," replied Mrs. Trueman. "But, surely their offences should not be visited on their poor wives, whose cup must already be full to running over. Instead of neglect and unkindness — their very position should make them objects of sympathy and active goodwill."

"Very true; but —" Mrs. Green paused. She was merely going to offer an excuse for her conduct; but felt that it would be far too transparent to affect the mind of Mrs. Trueman. She was embarrassed; and this embarrassment was plainly visible.

"We are too apt," resumed Mrs. Trueman, "to treat men who are addicted to intemperance as *criminals*, rather than as *invalids*."

"Invalids!" ejaculated Mary, in some surprise.

"Yes, invalids, for intemperance is a *disease* rather than a *crime*. The inebriate, ever impelled to the cup of intoxication by a *diseased appetite*, which he so often and earnestly strives to repress, needs *medicine* rather than *punishment*. But society too often visits with stripes, what can only yield to the physician's care, tenderness, and wise application of remedies. Will you pardon me, Mrs. Green, if I speak freely in the present case — if I seek to create in your mind a different regard for Mr. Striker than you now entertain? Believe me that I have only good in view. Shall I tell you the story that poor, sick Mrs. Striker told to me?"

"If you please," said Mrs. Green, in a low voice.

"I was so encouraged about my husband, a few weeks ago, said Mrs. Striker," thus began Mrs. Trueman; "he never had seemed so earnest in his life about giving up his bad habit of drinking. One morning — it was after a day on which two of our neighbors had quarreled with and fretted him until they drove him to the bottle, which he had promised never to touch again — we had a long talk, and he was in such real earnest about the matter, that my heart became full of hope. We shall have better days, Hannah, he repeated over and over again. I will be a *man* again. And with these words he left me for his shop. Oh, ma'am, my heart had not been so light for years, as it was during the whole of that morning. I felt that the unhappy past was no more to be repeated in the future. I was sure my husband was in earnest — in earnest as I had not seen him for a long, long time before. I even caught myself many times singing at my work, as I moved about the house; and wondered how it could be so. Ah! ma'am, how little did I dream of what was to follow. Noon came and passed — it was our dinner-hour — he was ever, when entirely himself, promptly at home as the line of shadow on the window marked the hour of twelve; but he was still away, and for the first time since morning, a gloom fell upon my spirit. Just then *Nancy Wimble* called in and told me that a writ had been served on my husband that morning at the direction of Mary Green. Oh, ma'am! How suddenly did my bright hopes go out in utter darkness. I comprehended all in a moment. My husband, worried and made angry by this, had fallen again, and from that day until this — he has scarcely drawn a sober breath. Strong in body, and cheerful in mind as I was that morning — both body and mind gave way in a moment. For days I was unable to lift my head from the pillow, and in all this time of sickness and sorrow, not a neighbor came in to see me, or to look after my poor neglected children. Oh, ma'am — I have wondered since, that my heart did not break —"

Mrs. Trueman paused, for a smothered sob, followed by a gush of tears, from Mary Green — told her that, in narrating what she had heard, the desired impression was made. A few moments sat Mrs. Green, struggling to calm herself. Failing in this, she started up suddenly, and, turning away, almost fled from the presence of Mrs. Trueman and her daughter.

The thoughts of the blacksmith had run somewhat clearer on that day, though he was exceedingly fretted in prospect of the trial to take place on the day following; and several times, as a sort of desperation came over him, he had thrown down his hammer and started for Joe Parker's tavern. Before reaching this place, however, better purposes each time gained power in his mind, and forced him back again to his shop. A new struggle had commenced; yet, even while he struggled in the powerful folds of a debased appetite, he had a sickening consciousness that, when the morrow came, even if he kept himself sober until then, the odds would all be on the adverse side. Whether the case of Mary Green went for or against him, in either event, the balance of reason would be disturbed — and he had a troubled foreboding of another, and, perhaps, lower fall.

Sobriety gave the blacksmith a clearer view of his social business and domestic relations, and this tended in no degree to soothe his troubled feelings. He was not earning enough to buy the food that was consumed at his table; and there was no rational prospect of a change for the better. Nearly all the work of Cedardale was going over to Elderglen, and the fires on his forge were dead, in consequence, for a larger portion of the time. Even as he was musing despondingly on this gloomy condition of things, White, the miller, rode by, with his bag of picks and facing-hammers, on his way to Elderglen; and, soon after, a neighboring farmer, from whom he had been in the habit of receiving a good deal of work, drove along past his shop in the same direction. At this, a feeling of anger and bitterness was mixed with the blacksmith's despondency.

A trifling job at which he had been working, being finished, Striker sat down upon his anvil, with no clearly defined train of thought in his mind; yet with a depressing weight on his feelings. This weight kept on increasing, until the unhappy man, unable passively to endure the pressure any longer, started up with an ejaculation of pain, at the same time that he struck his hands together with considerable force.

"O dear! I can't bear this. It will drive me mad!" he had just exclaimed, impatiently, when the sound of horses' hoofs and the voice of a man arrested his attention. Going to the door of his smithy, he was a little surprised to see *the stranger* whom, a short time previously, he had treated with so much discourtesy, in the act of dismounting. The man, after hitching his horse, came forward, and said, in a pleasant tone —

"Good-day, neighbor Striker. Can you do a little work for me?"

To this unexpected salutation, the blacksmith replied, in a manner very different indeed from that used on a former occasion —

"I shall be much pleased to serve you, sir."

"I have just moved into your neighborhood," said the man. "My name is *Trueman*. I have taken the old Markland house; and finding things a good deal out of repair, shall need considerable work done in your line. In riding down here, my horse has lost a shoe. So, if you will replace it now, I will be much obliged."

How instantly changed were the blacksmith's feelings! The pulses of his heart beat to a quicker measure; and the heavy weight he was a little while before so vainly endeavoring to throw off, fell, like the *burden of 'Christian'*, suddenly from his shoulders. With alacrity he stepped to the horse, examined his foot, took the dimensions, and was soon busy at his forge and anvil.

Meantime, Mr. Trueman took occasion to speak further of the work he wished done, and he asked the blacksmith a good many questions as to the state of affairs in the village. Striker's version did not place things in a very encouraging light. In referring to the miller, the shoemaker, and several others — he expressed himself very strongly, and said they might starve before he would turn his hand over to help them, or give them a stroke of his work. As for Mrs. Green, he denounced her bitterly. To all this, Mr. Trueman replied with as much prudence as was possible. Mrs. Green had, no doubt, been *badly advised*, he said, and he would take occasion to see and have a serious talk with her.

"Oh, don't see her on my account," replied Striker, quickly, to this suggestion. "I've no favors to ask of her. I wouldn't turn over my little finger to induce her to give up the suit. She's undertaken to drive me — so let her whip on. If she doesn't repent of this work before she's done with it, I'm mistaken. She's forgotten the damage I suffered from her cow in the destruction of my garden; but I haven't. That rod is over her head — though she little dreams of it; but it will fall — it will fall!"

And Striker fairly ground his teeth in his angry excitement.

"All this is wrong, my friend," said Mr. Trueman, mildly; "and two wrongs, as you have often heard it said, never make a right. Do you think you are a *happier* or a *better* man, since Mrs. Green commenced this suit?"

"Happier and better!" exclaimed the blacksmith, in some surprise at the singular question. Then after a pause, he said, with much feeling —

"Heaven knows that I am not. Happier and better? I am *worse* than I have ever been, and oh! *wretched* beyond endurance."

Mr. Trueman was deeply moved by the tone and manner in which this was uttered. He did not say a great deal more — except in a general way, but he made up his mind to see Mrs. Green at the earliest moment, and use his good offices toward effecting a settlement of the difficulty between her and the blacksmith. On leaving Mr. Striker, he requested him to call over at his house in the morning, as he wished to consult him about several matters in his line.

"I can't come in the morning," replied Striker. "But I will try and see you in the afternoon."

"Ah, very well. That will do. You have work in the morning?"

"Work!" There was bitterness in the blacksmith's tones. "Yes; and a precious job it is — more profit to the *lawyers* than to anyone else, by a great deal."

"Oh! That matter with Mrs. Green?"

"Yes. The trial takes place tomorrow morning."

Without making answer to this, Mr. Trueman rode off. He, too, had work to do, and he must be at it right early.

After Mr. Trueman left, Striker lingered at his shop for a short period, and then went home. Strongly was he tempted to turn aside into the tavern of Joe Parker; but his better resolution prevailed for the time, and he kept on his way. As he passed up the garden walk, he saw, through an open window, the back of a woman who appeared to be engaged in ironing. It was not his wife, and a momentary wonder as to who it could be passed through his mind. He caught a glimpse of the same figure as he entered the door, and went into the little sitting-room, where he found his wife at work, mending a garment for one of the children. There was a singular expression on her face; and the light which flashed over it as he entered, showed that something of more than common interest had occurred.

"Who is that?" Striker asked, in a low voice, pointing toward the door of the next room — for, with this woman, at whose figure he had merely glanced, he now connected the change in his wife's state of feelings.

"Mary Green," was answered, and with a smile that could not be repressed.

"What!" The voice of the blacksmith was stern, and a cloud fell instantly on his brow.

"Hush!" Mrs. Striker raised her finger. "You wouldn't guess what has happened," she said in a low, earnest voice. "But let me tell you. I was standing, about an hour ago, at the table in the kitchen, trying to iron a few things; but so weak and faint that it seemed as if every moment I would sink to the floor. Hearing someone open the gate, I looked out of the window, and you may believe that I was surprised when I saw Mary Green coming quickly up the walk. I began to tremble all over, and grew so much weaker, that I sunk down upon a chair, and remained in this way, with my hand still on the iron, when she came in. The moment she saw me she stood right still, and remained looking at me so long that I began to feel strange. At last she said —

"Oh, Mrs. Striker! can you ever forgive me for my cruelty and wicked neglect? What did come over me! I have surely not been myself!"

"I saw, now, that her eyes were red and her cheeks wet. I tried to answer, but could not. All was bewilderment. I wondered if I was not dreaming. But I did not wonder long. Mary came and sat down by me, and taking my hand, said, in that kind way she has —

"I have acted very wrong, Hannah, toward your husband, and

very wrong toward you. Him I have persecuted, and you neglected. But I was not myself. I opened my heart for wicked thoughts to come in, and they have ruled me. I was *badly advised*, and weak and foolish enough to act from my bad advisers. I repent now, Hannah, from my very heart, and I have come not only to ask forgiveness, but to do all in my power to repair the wrong. Will you, can you, forgive me?"

"If so weak before, John, that I could not stand, my strength was all gone now. I tried again to speak, but could not. I looked earnestly into Mary's face — *looked* my forgiveness, and then fell forward with my face upon her bosom. I had no further power to hold myself up. Tenderly she kissed me, and then drew her arms lovingly around me. The short time I lay thus, was a happy time, John."

The blacksmith had been for some moments, struggling with his feelings. Now he caught his breath several times, quickly, and dashed his hand across his eyes. But he made no reply.

"She had come," resumed Mrs. Striker, "so she said, not only to ask our forgiveness and to tell us that the suit should be stopped immediately, but to see if there was anything which, as a neighbor, she could do for me. The ironing-table, with its pile of clothes at which I was standing when she came in, soon attracted her notice.

"Ah, yes; I see what I can do for you," said she — "you haven't the strength for this." And so she went to work at the ironing, and insists on doing the whole of it for me before going home. It is indeed kind of her, John. And I'm sure you will forgive her, and I do, and let has-beens be has-beens. Won't you, John? You know she hasn't a bad heart. She was always so kind to me, before this, in sickness and in all times, John. Don't you know she was? And you always liked her. She's been badly advised, as she says. Won't you forgive her, John? Oh, I know you will."

"I am sure he will," said Mary Green, who had entered unperceived.

Both started and turned toward the door.

"John Striker, I have done you wrong, and repent; will you not forgive me?" said Mrs. Green, in a low, firm voice, and at the same time, she extended her hand toward the blacksmith.

"From my heart, Mary — from my heart!" replied the latter, with an emotion that he tried in vain to conceal.

"I forgive you as I hope to be forgiven for the many wrongs I have myself done."

There was light again in the blacksmith's humble dwelling; and a new hope in the heart of his longsuffering wife.

CHAPTER 13

On the morning after the reconciliation between Mary Green and the blacksmith's family, Striker went to his shop as sober as he had ever been in his life. The promise of work from Mr. Trueman kept his mind from sinking into a state of despondency, in view of the altered condition of things in Cedardale. After kindling his fires, and making up two or three light articles of domestic use, for which he hoped to find a sale, he took off his apron, and was preparing to go, as promised, to the house of Mr. Trueman, when, no little to his surprise, he saw Mr. White, the miller, approaching from the road, carrying in his hands a crowbar and a small wrench, both of which were broken, and an axe which his practiced eye told him at a glance required "setting."

There was in the manner of Mr. White, as he came up to the blacksmith, a clearly expressed doubt as to his reception. He bowed slightly and said, as he paused at the shop-door —

"Good morning."

"Good morning," returned Striker. He did not smile, nor was there a decided welcome in his countenance. But he was much subdued, and exhibited nothing repellant.

"Are you busy this morning?" asked the miller.

"Not particularly so," replied Striker. "I was about going over to see Mr. Trueman, who had several jobs in my way that he wants done."

"Ah, yes. He'll need a good deal of work done, no doubt," remarked Mr. White. "He seems like a clever man."

The blacksmith made no response to this. There was a moment or two of silence, which was broken by the miller, who said —

"I'd like you to mend this wrench and crowbar for me."

The blacksmith, as ready as he was to make up with the miller, wished to avoid seeming too eager to meet his overtures. Instead of showing at once the real pleasure he felt, and letting his willingness to serve him speak out in fitting words, he merely reached forth his hand and took the wrench and crowbar, which he carefully examined for a few moments, wondering within himself, while doing so, what could be the meaning of this change in the miller.

"We'll soon make these all right again," he remarked at length, in a pleasant voice — more pleasant, in fact, than he had designed it should be; and turning to his forge as he spoke, he thrust the two broken ends of the crowbar into the fire, and grasping the handle of the bellows, sent the sparks and blaze roaring up the chimney.

"How soon shall I call up for them?" now asked the miller.

"In about half an hour," replied Striker.

"You can set this at your leisure," said Mr. White, as he passed his fingers over the worn and battered edge of the old axe, which he had thrown aside more than a year ago, but which was now brought forth to the light, more for the blacksmith's benefit than his own.

"I'll do it for you today or tomorrow," returned Striker.

"That will be fine," was the miller's response.

Both the men felt, during this time, no little embarrassment. The blacksmith was pleased that the miller had come; and the miller was pleased to meet with a reception more gracious than he had expected. The latter was still lingering in the smithy, hurriedly debating with himself as to whether it would be prudent to say certain things that were in his mind, touching their late misunderstanding, when he observed *Nancy Wimble* passing along the road, with her usual quick step, and air of one who has something of importance to communicate. Striker saw her at the same moment, and he remarked with considerable feeling —

"That woman has done more harm in Cedardale than she will ever repair, if she lives a hundred years!"

"You may well affirm that," was the miller's feeling response. "And now that we have spoken of her, I might as well come out plainly, and say why I called on you in the angry way I did, a few weeks ago. It was in consequence of something that *she* told me."

"What did she tell you?" said the blacksmith, resting on his bellows, and manifesting considerable interest.

"Why, she told me that Mrs. Striker said I had two spouts running from the millstones, and, in that way, double-tolled every grist I ground."

"Nancy Wimble told you that!" exclaimed the blacksmith, advancing from his forge a pace or two, and exhibiting a good deal of excitement.

"Yes, she did; or, at least, gave me to understand that Mrs. Striker had said something of the kind — and I couldn't stand that, nohow."

Before Striker replied to this, he remembered that his wife had complained, more than once, of light weight, after having been to the mill; and comprehending how readily, in gossiping with *Nancy*, she might have been betrayed into expressions which the latter could distort and exaggerate, he checked on his lips an indignant denial, and remained silent for some moments. He was struggling for self-possession. At length, he was able to speak calmly, and he said —

"If my wife had thought this, I am sure she would have said so to me."

"And she never did?"

"Never, Mr. White," replied the blacksmith earnestly. "Never, I do assure you."

"Enough. I was wrong, very wrong, to come as I did, in hot blood, on the mere *allegation* of Nancy Wimble. Oh, she is a desperate mischief-maker!"

"I know it — I know it," said the blacksmith with feeling.

"Did she repeat to you or Mrs. Striker anything that I said?" asked the miller.

"She did; and if you said what she repeated, Mr. White, they were hard words — very hard words."

The blacksmith showed no anger; he spoke rather as one whose feelings had been deeply wounded.

"I did speak harshly and unguardedly, I know," said the miller, with that frankness of acknowledgment usually found in men of hasty temper, "but then, I was dreadfully provoked at what Nancy said. How could I help being so?"

"And I was provoked also, friend White," the blacksmith answered promptly. "When I saw tears in Hannah's eyes, and heard from her lips what you said of us — *Nancy* had told her — you will not now wonder that I was angry, when you came to me as you did. It wasn't for myself that I cared. But Hannah — poor soul! She had enough to bear as it was. Ah me!"

The blacksmith's feelings partially overcame him; and he stopped suddenly, but not before the miller perceived how much he was disturbed.

"Let us be friends again, Mr. Striker," said the latter, reaching forth his hand.

"With all my heart," replied the blacksmith. "It is always best to forgive and forget."

And the two men joined hands and shook them heartily. A pleasant little chat followed, then they parted, both feeling happier than they had felt for many weeks.

While the blacksmith was wondering within himself as to what had wrought so unexpected a change in the miller, (he did not know that Mr. Trueman had been at the mill with half a dozen bags of grain late on the preceding day,) Wimble, the shoemaker, who had broken a hammer, which he could not dispense with so long a time as it would require to send over to Elderglen, came in with evident reluctance, and a doubt as to the reception he would meet.

Striker had cause enough to be angry toward the shoemaker; but choking down his feelings, and saying — "Let has-beens be has-beens," he received him with at least a show of welcome.

"Can you mend this hammer for me?" asked Wimble.

"I reckon so," replied the blacksmith.

"How soon can you have it done?"

"Sometime today," was answered.

"I need it this morning. It's one I am using all the while, and I cannot get along without it."

"I'm sorry," said Striker. "But as soon as I can get this wrench and crowbar mended, I must go over to Mr. Trueman's. I promised to call there this morning, and would have done so before this, if Mr. White hadn't come in with these to mend."

"Humph! White!" The shoemaker's look and tone were most contemptuous. "I thought you'd had enough of him. And this Trueman, too. I suppose you're going to toady to him, like all the rest of Cedardale. Humph! I gave you, at least, credit for more spirit than this."

Striker had taken the broken hammer in his hand, and was already examining the fracture, and calculating the time it would require to mend it.

But the shoemaker's words so roused his indignation, that, on the impulse of the moment, he threw the hammer out into the road, saying as he did so, angrily —

"There's a blacksmith in Elderglen; and he's as good a workman today as he was last week. Take your hammer there. And hark! If, from this day forth, you speak to me an ill word of anybody in Cedardale, I'll get up a cry against you, that will drive you and your mischief-making wife, bag and baggage from the village!"

It may well be supposed that Wimble was no little astonished by so unexpected a rebuff as this. He turned away while yet the blacksmith was speaking, for he was a coward at heart, as all such people are. Still further surprised was he, as he did so, to find himself almost face to face with Mr. Trueman, who had entered the smithy just in time to hear Striker's closing words.

"Softly — softly, good friends," said Mr. Trueman, with a mild dignity that produced an instant pause in the storm. Then he added, "That was a pretty hard saying of yours, neighbor Striker." And he looked at the blacksmith with an expression which said, "I had hoped better things of you."

"You wouldn't much wonder at me, I am sure, Mr. Trueman," replied the blacksmith in a voice now fallen to a subdued and somewhat deprecating tone, "if you knew the cause of my anger against Wimble; you have no doubt learned, before this, he and his wife are at the bottom of nearly all the trouble at Cedardale! And now just as my heart was warming toward you as a real friend, and just as White and myself had shaken hands and forgiven each other — in he comes, and tries to blow up another *fire of discord!* Do you wonder, after all I have been and suffered, that I was angry?"

There was an *honest indignation* about Striker that had its effect on Mr. Trueman, as well as on Wimble. The effect on each, however, was very different. While Mr. Trueman's face assumed a grave, almost severe aspect, and his form grew more and more erect, the shoemaker looked abashed and seemed to shrink into himself.

"I am afraid," said Mr. Trueman, addressing Wimble, and speaking with some severity, "that you and your family have been much to blame for the *unhappy differences* which have for some time existed in Cedardale. This is the testimony I hear borne against you on all sides; and I am only the more surprised that, knowing you as well as they do, your neighbors have ever permitted themselves to be influenced against each other by your *tattling* and *slanderous* propensities. I speak to you plainly, because I think *plain talk* is best in a case like yours; and because I wish you to know in the beginning, that I perfectly understand you and the estimation in which you are held. I am, as you are aware, a new-comer, and I expect to reside in this neighborhood for many years, perhaps for my whole lifetime. I like *peace and harmony* in my own dwelling, and peace and harmony all around me. I could no more live among quarreling neighbors, than I could live in a quarreling family. If there is discord around me, I can never rest until order is restored. As it is with me, so it is with every member of my family. You and your family, it seems, feel and act differently. Now, the influence of either the one or the other must have sway. Which shall it be? I'm rather a self-willed man, friend Wimble" — Mr. Trueman spoke more pleasantly — "and, when I take my course, am very apt to persevere to the end, no matter what difficulties arise. So, if you mean to contend with me for influence in Cedardale, you must make up your mind for a pretty hard contest. What do you say?" and Mr. Trueman now smiled, and spoke with a kind of soft persuasion, "hadn't you better come over to my side? I would rather, a thousand times, have you for a friend than an enemy."

Wimble, who was rather a weak-minded man, felt completely knocked down, so to speak, by this harangue, so unexpected, so condemnatory, so mortifying. He tried to stammer out some answer, but was unable to utter a coherent sentence.

"Are you doing as well now as you were a few months ago, Mr. Wimble?" asked Mr. Trueman, changing his manner and tone of voice altogether.

"No, sir," replied the shoemaker.

"Why not?"

"More than half the work is going over to Elderglen."

"Indeed! How is that?"

"People think they get better work there, perhaps."

"Didn't I see you at the blacksmith's over there, last week?"

"You did."

"Was the work better done there?"

"I don't say that it was," answered Wimble, a little fretfully.

"You had a bag of grain with you," pursued Mr. Trueman. "Was it better ground than our Cedardale miller can grind it?"

Wimble was silent.

"I don't think you can say so," pursued Mr. Trueman. "I am sure you cannot say so. Then what did you gain? Nothing. But what did you lose? That is a more serious question. There was not only loss of time, but loss of two customers, as well as loss of neighborly interest and good-will. Don't you know that a house divided against itself cannot stand? Neither can a village divided against itself stand. Nobody seems to be doing well in Cedardale. Why? Because almost everyone is at variance with his neighbor; and almost everyone, in consequence, running over to Elderglen. From all I can learn, Mr. Wimble — forgive my exceeding plainness of speech — you and your family are to blame in a great measure for this result; and, not escaping the evil which has fallen upon the rest, you are yourselves now among the sufferers."

The shoemaker looked very much humiliated, and did not attempt to defend himself, for his conscience too surely confirmed the accusations so pointedly brought against him.

"Are you willing to be at peace again with your neighbors?" asked Mr. Trueman.

"Oh, yes, certainly, if they will be at peace with me. But I don't see much chance for that," replied Wimble.

"Why not?"

"Martin has sued me."

"The schoolmaster?"

"Yes."

"Ah! what's the meaning of that?"

"A suit for slander, I believe," said the blacksmith.

"Oh! is that all? A very easy matter to settle," replied Mr. Trueman. "I must see Martin. How is his school now?"

"He hasn't much school left to brag about," said Wimble quickly, and with evident pleasure in his voice.

"Not much to brag about!" And Mr. Trueman fixed his eyes so steadily upon the shoemaker, that the gaze of the latter fell to the ground, while a slight flush of shame came to his face. "Does your son go to him?"

"No, indeed! My boy shall never darken his schoolroom door again," replied Wimble, with considerable warmth.

"Don't say that. Let me ask you a question." There was something so serious in Mr. Trueman's manner, that Wimble felt a momentary concern. The former, after a pause, approached the shoemaker, and stooping to his ear, said —

"Would you rather have your son darken Martin's school-room door, or the door of a county prison?"

There was a significance in the manner of Trueman not to be mistaken. Wimble started, and turning pale, asked hurriedly, yet in a low voice —

"For mercy's sake, sir! what do you mean?"

Taking the shoemaker by the arm, Mr. Trueman passed with him from the shop, and so soon as they were a few paces from the door, said —

"Let me show you the consequence of some of your own acts. You, or your wife, it matters not for our present purpose which, got up a quarrel between the miller and the blacksmith. So the miller takes his work over to Elderglen, and sends his son for it when ready. Your son sees him riding over, and reports, falsely, to the schoolmaster, that young White had played the truant. Martin, believing this story, flogs White severely; at which his father quarrels with Martin, and takes his son from school. The base and cruel falsehood of your boy becoming fully known to the schoolmaster, he punishes him, as he deserves, and you, instead of approving this, also quarrel with Martin, and take your son from under his care. What is the result? *Idleness is the parent of vice.* Twice during the short period that has gone by since we removed into the neighborhood, have I found your son trespassing on my place; and this morning I caught him in my chicken-house with more than a dozen eggs in his hat, which he had taken from my nests. Nor was this all: he had wrung the neck of one of my choicest breed of hens, and had the dead body under his arm, when I came suddenly upon him. Do you understand my question now, Mr. Wimble? I will repeat it: Would you rather have your son darken Mr. Martin's school-room door — or the door of a county prison? For, unless I am very much mistaken, he will enter either the one or the other."

Just then the shoemaker's wife, who had been on a flying visit to one of the few neighbors with whom she was on good terms, came past on her way home. Wimble was now thoroughly alarmed at the new aspect in which things were presented to him. His mind, never very strong or clear, was all in confusion.

"Nancy! Nancy! here!" he called to his wife, who was going by without stopping.

"Say over to her, Mr. Trueman, will you, what you have just said to me," he added, as soon as Nancy came up.

Mr. Trueman did not hesitate to comply with the shoemaker's wishes. He merely stepped back to say to Mr. Striker that he would like to see him at his house in an hour, and then walked away with John and Nancy Wimble.

CHAPTER 14

A week more, and the change in Cedardale was indeed remarkable. It might almost be said that the lion had lain down with the lamb.

No light task had Mr. Trueman and his excellent family, in accomplishing this work; but, having silenced — almost paralyzed — the shoemaker and his wife by meeting their case in the very prompt manner just related, they found the main difficulties removed, and soon had the pleasure of seeing the road to Elderglen in a measure deserted.

Martin, the schoolmaster, who was already beginning to see *haggard want* approaching his little family, did not require much prompting to induce him to withdraw the suit which had been commenced against the Wimbles, nor was persuasion needed to cause the Wimbles to send Dick back to school. The revelations of Mr. Trueman, and the severe lesson he read them after they all retired from the blacksmith's shop, both alarmed and humbled them.

At first, some two or three of the leading families in Cedardale, when the evil work of the shoemaker and his wife was fairly set forth to view, indignantly declared, that unless they were driven "bag and baggage," as the blacksmith had said, out of the village, there was no hope of quiet in the future. This idea getting current, was pondered over and over, and there was a short period when several parties stubbornly declared that, "It was no use to talk — the Wimbles must leave the village. They were at the bottom of the late trouble; and it was vain to hope for peace and harmony while they remained."'

"I rather think," was the answer of both Mr. Trueman and his wife to this, "that if there had not been a willingness in Cedardale to *hear* evil things spoken against neighbors, the Wimbles would soon have found mischief-making a rather dull business."

This remark, not very flattering to the self-love of some who heard it, tended to silence the more forward advocates of expulsion, and to allow the better views of the case presented by the Truemans to prevail.

"Let everyone," said they, "turn a deaf ear to the busybody, the talebearer, and the mischief-maker — and no harm can be done. Wimble is a good shoemaker; take his shoes, and reject his ill-news, if he offers to tell any. And, above all, be more ready to believe a good, than an evil report of your neighbor."

So it was finally settled that, for their past misdoings, the extreme punishment threatened should not be visited on the Wimbles.

Soon the blacksmith's forge was in blast from the rising to the setting of the sun; the great mill-wheel revolved unceasingly; the shoemaker had so much work to do, that he had no time to meddle with his neighbor's concerns; and the schoolmaster looked down from his desk upon full benches; while the storekeeper, who had begun seriously to think of moving to Elderglen, quite gave up that notion. The only one in Cedardale who did not prosper and become happier in consequence of the Truemans' good offices, was Joe Parker, the tavern-keeper, who never spoke a good word in regard to them. But his influence in the village was now of small account.

Perhaps the most gratifying result of all this was the fact that Striker, now more kindly, and therefore more wisely treated by his neighbors, never after relapsed into his old ways, but became thoroughly reformed, and in a few years was able to buy the snug little house he had long occupied with his family as a rent-paying tenant.

As there is nothing more of interest to relate, we must now close this little history of village life. Cedardale, freed from internal strife, showed year after year new signs of prosperity. The Truemans never lost their influence, which was always exercised for good; and their example shows how a single family or individual in a community, if true-hearted and right-minded — may effectually counteract the evil-doing of the envious, and the ill-natured, and the mischief-making, and even bring harmony out of jarring discord.

CPSIA information can be obtained
at www.ICGtesting.com
Printed in the USA
FFOW01n0948160916
27732FF